Their Forbidden Storm

Christina Diane

Their Forbidden Storm

Edited by Emily Lawrence at Lawrence Editing

Contents

Dedication

For those who dare to dream bigger, love harder, and refuse to settle for the ordinary. Here's to the ones who make their own rules, follow their own path, and embrace the beautiful chaos of it all. You know who you are, and you're exactly who you were meant to be.

Note to Readers

Thank you so much for picking up my book—I'm truly delighted (and doing an undignified happy dance) that you're here!

Before we step into the historical world of Christina Diane, I wanted to share a little something about what to expect. While my books are set in the Regency era, I write with the modern reader in mind. You can expect stories that are character-driven, fast-paced, and heavy on the spice, with lively dialogue and plenty of heart.

I do my best to capture the setting and language of the time through research, but strict historical accuracy isn't my primary goal. Sometimes my characters insist on doing and speaking things their own way—and I let them. So, if you're looking for meticulous period detail and perfect historical precision, this book may not be what you are looking for (and that's completely okay!).

But if you're here for passionate heroines, swoonworthy gentlemen, witty banter, high stakes, high heat, and happily ever afters, all wrapped in a Regency-inspired world that welcomes diverse, bold, and intriguing characters—you're in the right place.

I hope this story sweeps you off your feet and carries you into a world of romance, tension, and a touch of scandal.

Much love and swoon,

CHRISTINA
DIANE

Content Warnings

This book doesn't dive deep into the dark stuff—but you might encounter boundary-challenged relatives, oversharing friends, and a generous dash of spice. I aim to flag anything that might need a warning, but if I miss something, send me a message so I can update the list for future readers. To keep this message spoiler-free, you can check out identified content warnings here: https://christinadianebooks.com/content-warnings/

Prologue

Kent, England - Summer, 1815: Lucy

Lady Lucy Lygon had never been happier to return home to Ashburn Manor after a miserable London Season. Yet, the reason for that misery had followed her home.

Her parents.

She believed they loved her—as much as a duke and duchess who valued titles and society above all else could. They had, at least, agreed not to force her into marriage during her first season. Small favors. Yet she knew that reprieve might not last. Sooner or later, they would insist she marry a man of their choosing. At least they would be choosy; perhaps, in the time it took, Lucy might find someone who stirred her heart. But if the crop of men cluttering London ballrooms was any indication, she doubted it.

Not that her choice would matter, anyway. Her parents had their own criteria—title and connections far outweighed something as trivial as love.

After breakfast in her room, Lucy practically flew down the stairs, eager to visit her horse, Thor, after months away. Just as she reached the terrace door, her mother's voice clipped through the air.

"Lucy, darling."

Lucy froze and turned with deliberate slowness to face the Duchess of Ashburn. "Yes, Mother?"

"We have guests for tea this afternoon. Please be presentable."

Her mother's disapproval was palpable. She hated that Lucy preferred the company of horses to mingling with her mother's haughty friends.

"I'll bathe after my ride," Lucy promised, resisting the urge to roll her eyes. She supposed she did smell rather like a stable after a long ride.

"Very well," her mother sighed, turning on her heel in a gesture that ended the conversation.

Lucy hurried outside, the sun heating her face as she made her way to the stables. The familiar scent of hay and leather greeted her, warm and comforting. She went straight to Thor, running her fingers along his powerful neck.

"Would you like him saddled, my lady?" a rich baritone asked from behind her.

The deep voice sent a shiver down her spine. She turned and met the gaze of a man who was, quite simply, breathtaking. Chiseled jaw, piercing emerald eyes, and thick chestnut hair that fell just a touch too long. His rolled-up sleeves revealed muscular forearms dusted with dark hair. Her mouth went dry, and all coherent thought left her entirely.

"My lady?" he asked again, his brow creased with concern. "Did you wish to take your horse out?"

"Yes," Lucy managed, swallowing hard, her voice barely above a whisper. Proud of herself that she had even managed the single word.

"I'll have him ready for you in just a moment."

Then he grinned at her.

It hit her like a lightning strike—sharp, sudden, and impossible to ignore. That grin. It unraveled her. His features softened, and in his eyes, she glimpsed something rare...kindness. No posturing lord, no false airs—just a man, genuine and unguarded. Something in her trusted him, believed in him, though she barely knew him at all.

She stepped back and watched him work. The flex of muscle beneath his shirt as he lifted the saddle, the deft way his hands buckled each strap—it was mesmerizing. Now she understood how a woman could become wanton. Her cheeks heated at the thought.

When he finished, he walked Thor to the mounting block and extended a hand to help her up. The moment her gloved fingers met his, heat flared through her veins. Even the fabric between them couldn't dull the sensation.

He swallowed hard, his throat bobbing. Had he felt it too?

"I didn't catch your name," Lucy said, her voice unsteady.

"Jones, my lady," he replied softly, still holding her hand. "Mister Jones."

She stared into those green eyes, unable to pull away. For a foolish moment, she imagined what it might be like if they weren't bound by their places in the world.

"And what should I call you?" Jones asked, his thumb brushing the back of her hand.

Her breath caught. She wanted to tell him to call her Lucy. Just Lucy. His Lucy. But if her parents so much as suspected a hint of familiarity, Jones would lose his position in an instant.

"Lady Lucy," she said softly.

His expression shuttered. He released her hand and stepped back. "The duke's daughter," he murmured, half to himself.

"Yes," she said, already missing the warmth of his touch.

Jones nodded stiffly. "I hope you enjoy your ride, my lady."

Her heart twisted painfully at the shift in his tone. It was ridiculous. They'd barely exchanged a handful of words. But she'd felt something—something real, something undeniable.

She mounted Thor and, without looking back, galloped across the meadow. The wind stung her cheeks, but she barely noticed.

Fool. For once, she'd felt something more than duty and obligation—more than the dull, tedious world her parents had prepared for her. But whatever spark she'd found with Jones, she knew it could never be.

Lucy was the dutiful daughter—obedient in action, rebellious in thought. This would be no different. She could look, she could dream of a life with a handsome groom, but that was all it could ever be. No one could ever know.

And she could only hope that someday, a man from her own world might stir even a fraction of the longing she'd felt in that fleeting moment with Jones. Because what other choice did she have?

Chapter 1

Kent, England - Summer, 1817: Lucy

Lucy swallowed her irritation, but the sharp edge of it simmered beneath her skin. She knew what was coming. Her mother's scolding followed a familiar pattern, always laced with that particular tone—one that dripped with disappointment.

"Lucy, darling," her mother began, her voice coated in condescension, "you simply must make an effort during our house party. There will be suitable lords in attendance, and Lord Rutherford has expressed a particular interest—"

No. Not again. Not Rutherford. Not this lecture.

"Excuse me, Mother. I'll just be a moment." Lucy shot up from the settee.

"Lucy, we are not finished—"

But Lucy was already gone, her heart hammering as she bolted from the room. She quickened her pace, desperate to outrun her mother's relentless expectations. Fuck that.

In her mind, she could scream all the vulgar curses she swallowed in silence. In her mind, she was bold, defiant—free. Out here in the world, she played the part they demanded: the perfect, beautiful daughter of a duke.

But in her mind, she could dream. And they couldn't control her mind.

When would it end? When she wed some arrogant lord with a title to match her father's ambitions? No. Even then, she would still be a pawn—a beautiful, smiling figure in someone else's game. And that was the role that would break her.

If only her brother were home from his Grand Tour. He'd have stood by her, kept their parents from forcing her into a match she didn't want. Threatened Rutherford to leave her alone. But he wasn't here. And their father always got what he wanted.

She was lucky they hadn't forced her hand already. But their patience was waning—Lord Rutherford's name constantly discussed, a reminder that time was slipping away.

Thank God Margot would arrive soon. Her cousin's sharp tongue and scandalous behavior made Lucy feel braver, bolder. Lucy envied her—envied the way Margot did whatever she pleased, without apology.

Once outside, Lucy inhaled deeply, the fresh air cutting through her irritation. Her favorite place lay just ahead—the stables. Everyone believed it was her love of horses that drew her there. But, in truth, that was only part of it.

It was him.

Gathering her skirts, she broke into a run.

Her breath came in uneven gasps by the time she reached the stables. Empty. Disappointment tugged at her chest. She approached Thor's stall, pressing her fingers to his warm muzzle.

Thor nickered softly, nudging her palm in greeting. Lucy leaned her forehead against his neck, closing her eyes.

She wanted more—more than vacant suitors chasing her for what they deemed as assets, more than a life dictated by rules and expectations. More than a husband chosen to secure alliances instead of affection.

She wanted him.

For two years, she had carried her torment. Watching him. Finding excuses to cross his path, to steal a moment in his presence. He made her feel seen, not as a duke's daughter, but as herself. She could laugh with him, tease him. He listened, really listened, in a way no one else did. But did it mean anything to him?

Her fingers curled into Thor's mane, her throat tightening.

Because the cruelest part?

Even knowing it was hopeless... she still wanted him.

Her parents would never allow it. The world would shun them. Not that she truly cared about any of that. If he loved her, she would fight. Rail against the walls of her cage. But she wasn't even certain if the man felt anything for her at all.

But she didn't even know if he felt anything for her at all. And that uncertainty hurt most of all.

Sighing, she patted Thor again, picturing Jones in her mind. She'd long since lost count of the ways she'd imagined his lips on hers—the endless nights spent awake, aching for him.

You must stop this. The thought came often, a futile reprimand. She had tried to dismiss her feelings as infatuation, a passing fancy. But that was a lie—one she could no longer believe. Not when her mother was determined to push Rutherford into her path.

If her mother had even the faintest inkling of Lucy's thoughts, or what she did alone in her chamber, whispering Jones' name into the dark as her hands roamed her body—well, the duchess would surely succumb to a fit of apoplexy.

Her parents wanted Lord Rutherford for her—a man of wealth, status, and good breeding. They'd actually said that. Good breeding. Yet when Lucy closed her eyes at night, it was never Rutherford's face she saw.

It was always his.

Fool that she was, Lucy's gaze flicked to the stable doors, heart pounding with the desperate, unspoken hope that he might appear.

And then—he did.

Jones entered, carrying a saddle slung over one shoulder. His chestnut hair was tousled, a few locks falling across his brow. His emerald eyes glinted in the afternoon light, and Lucy's breath caught.

"Good afternoon, Lady Lucy," he said, his voice low and rich. "We've been preparing for your family's guests."

She swallowed hard, willing her breath to return. "I wondered where everyone was," she lied.

"Out exercising the horses." He placed the saddle on its rack, then glanced back at her. "I didn't expect to see you here. I thought you'd be busy with the party preparations."

"I… needed some air," she said, still gripping Thor's mane like a lifeline. Even the man's voice impacted every inch of her body.

Jones moved closer, each step narrowing the unbearable space between them. The scent of leather clung to him, mingling with something distinctly, intoxicatingly him. It made her dizzy. Reckless even.

"Is everything all right, my lady?" His voice was softer now, laced with concern.

Her carefully constructed mask slipped. He always had that effect on her. Every. Single. Time. Around him, she couldn't pretend to be someone she wasn't. She had only ever wanted him to see her truest self.

"No," she admitted. "My parents are determined to marry me off, and I fear they've set their sights on Lord Rutherford." Her voice faltered. "And I don't think I can bear it."

She risked a glance at him then, searching his face for… something. Disapproval. Pity. Maybe even jealousy.

But Jones gave nothing away. His gaze held hers, steady and intent, unreadable but warm. Damn him.

He leaned against Thor's stall, close enough that Lucy felt the warmth of his body. Too close.

"It's a heavy burden you carry," Jones said softly.

A bitter laugh escaped her lips as her fingers absently traced Thor's mane. "You have no idea."

How could he? Even as a servant, he had choices—more freedom than she was afforded. "It would be easier if I weren't the daughter of a duke. If I could choose a husband for…"

Her voice faltered, heat crawling up her neck.

"For what, my lady?" His voice was low, coaxing.

She swallowed hard. "Love."

The word lingered between them, heavy with all the things she couldn't say. Her gaze dipped to his lips—a mistake. His mouth was far too tempting.

"From what I know of you," he murmured, his voice impossibly gentle, "I'm quite certain you would be easy to love."

Her breath hitched.

Did he just…? No. Surely she'd imagined it. She blinked, and he was still there, watching her with an intensity that left her breathless.

"Tell me," she whispered, her throat tight. "If you were in my position… what would you do?"

Jones kicked off the wall, stepping closer. Again, he was far too close. His breath warmed her cheek, his presence a magnetic pull she couldn't resist.

She could kiss him. Just one step forward, a tilt of her head, and she'd know. If this fire between them was foolish longing… or something far worse. Because she couldn't marry another man feeling as she did for him.

His gaze dropped to her lips. His hands clenched at his sides as though he were waging war with himself.

This might be her only chance.

Before she could second-guess herself, she reached for him, fisting his shirt and pulling him down. Her lips met his in a reckless, desperate kiss.

For a moment, nothing happened. Then his hands found her waist, strong and sure, gripping her as though she might slip away. His mouth moved against hers—hesitant at first, then demanding. Heat surged through her, robbing her of breath and reason. Her body melted against his, her heart hammering wildly in her chest.

And just as quickly, he tore himself away.

His chest heaved, hands raised in surrender. "My lady," he rasped, voice ragged. "I… that was…" He swallowed hard. "Please forgive me."

Forgive him? She could barely think past the blood pounding in her ears.

"I kissed you," she managed, mortification burning her face.

"And I shouldn't have returned it." His voice was rough, strained. "Shouldn't have put my hands on you."

His words stung, but her eyes drifted downward—and there it was. The undeniable strain in his breeches.

Heat pooled between her thighs, knowing she had undone him. Whatever noble restraint he clung to, his body betrayed him.

"But did you want to kiss me?" Her heart hammered in her chest, awaiting his response.

His breath faltered, his gaze locking onto hers. It was dark, smoldering, as well as raw and unguarded. His fingers flexed at his sides, like he was fighting the urge to reach for her again.

"Lady Lucy," he said, voice hoarse, "if we're caught... your family would give me the sack. And you have gentlemen arriving—men far more—"

"And yet you are the one I want." The words escaped before she could stop them.

He flinched as though she had struck him.

But she wasn't finished. Stepping forward, she looped her arms around his neck, pressing her body flush against his. "I can't stop thinking about you. And I'm tired of pretending."

His eyes closed, his jaw flexing tightly. Yet still, he didn't pull away.

"Please," she whispered, voice trembling. "Kiss me. Truly kiss me. And if you feel nothing... if you tell me this is all in my head, I'll never bother you again."

A low, tormented growl rumbled in his chest. "Damn it," he ground out.

Then he seized her, his mouth crashing down on hers in a kiss that she felt throughout her entire body.

This was no tentative meeting of lips—it was fire. His tongue traced the seam of her mouth, and when she parted for him, he deepened the kiss with a hunger that stole her reason. His fingers dug into her hips, pulling her closer.

Lucy arched into him, fisting his hair, desperate to be even closer. Desperate to drown in him. He groaned low in his throat, a sound that sent liquid heat pooling between her thighs.

And then—footsteps. Rapid, purposeful.

"Lady Lucy?" a familiar voice called out. "Are you here?"

Chapter 2

Lucy

Lucy sprang away from Jones a second before her lady's maid, Sarah, burst into the stables.

The maid's eyes widened, flicking between Lucy and Jones. Even without seeing them kiss, she knew.

"Begging your pardon, my lady," Sarah said in a rush, "but the first of the house party guests have arrived. Your mother sent me to fetch you immediately."

Lucy's stomach twisted. That kiss—that kiss—had set her entire world spinning, and now she was expected to smile and curtsy like nothing had happened. "Of course," she said, her voice hollow. As if she had a choice.

Turning to leave, Lucy dared one last glance at Jones. The longing she saw in his eyes mirrored her own, or at least she thought it did.

He gave her a small polite nod, a gesture that summed up what their entire relationship was supposed to be.

Each step away from him grew heavier, the weight of expectation settling over her like a suffocating cloak.

Once Lucy appeared back inside the house, her mother's sharp gaze swept over her, taking in her windblown hair and dirt-smeared gown.

"Lucy," the duchess said, voice cold enough to frost glass. "I see you've been wasting time with that horse instead of ensuring you look your best to receive our guests. Just look at yourself." Her eyes narrowed. "Dirt on your gown. How very undignified."

Lucy fought the urge to shrink under her mother's disapproval. "I just needed a moment to myself." And she ended up with far more than that.

"That's all well and good," her mother snapped, "but it won't secure Lord Rutherford. And that, my dear, should be your concern. Up to your chamber now. Sarah will make you presentable before Lord Rutherford arrives."

Lucy bit her tongue and climbed the stairs, feeling like a prisoner being marched to the gallows.

In her chamber, Sarah helped her into a fresh gown and began taming her hair. The silence between them stretched until Sarah spoke, voice hesitant.

"My lady… if I may… it seemed as if I interrupted something back there. In the stables." Her fingers faltered in Lucy's hair. "You know you shouldn't be alone with him."

Lucy's cheeks flamed. She fought the instinct to touch her lips, still tingling from Jones's kiss. "I was just visiting Thor."

Sarah's expression remained unconvinced. "I know you hate all this," she said quietly, "but these matchmaking efforts… they're for your own good. A proper marriage will provide you with security. Standing."

"You sound like my mother," Lucy muttered, fighting back tears. "Why must I pretend to be someone I'm not, Sarah?"

Sarah's gaze softened. "It's just… the way of things," she said with quiet sadness. "You are of their world. And servants, like myself and Mr. Jones, are of ours."

Lucy wasn't sure what flickered across Sarah's face then. Pity, warning, or something else entirely. But it left her unsettled.

Several moments later, Lucy found herself standing at the entrance to Ashburn Manor, a brittle smile plastered on her face. Another carriage rolled to a stop, and the blond-haired man who stepped out needed no introduction.

Lord Rutherford.

Chin high, chest puffed—he was every bit the preening aristocrat she had expected. Lucy rolled her eyes while no one was looking.

"Lord Rutherford," her mother cooed, casting a pointed look at Lucy. "We are delighted you joined us. I'm certain you will find the week's events most diverting."

Lord Rutherford smiled, more a smug curl of his lips than anything warm or genuine. He was handsome, in a way—a striking jaw, broad shoulders beneath his tailored coat, and breeches that shamelessly flaunted muscular thighs. And no doubt he knew it.

His reputation preceded him—a string of mistresses and a heart colder than ice.

When he approached Lucy, his gaze crawled over her in a way that made her stomach turn.

"Lady Lucy," he drawled, taking her hand. The glint in his eye was far too familiar—predatory, like a cat toying with a cornered mouse. His lips brushed her gloved knuckles, and Lucy resisted the urge to snatch her hand away.

"I look forward to getting to know you better," he said, voice oily and smug.

"Indeed, my lord," she forced out. She barely suppressed a shudder, already plotting how to spend as little time as possible in his company.

Her father's sharp cough snapped her back to reality, his glare pinning her in place. Dutifully, she forced her smile wider—her mother's version of perfection.

But beneath it, Lucy felt something stronger rise. Defiance.

Her thoughts strayed to Jones—to the warmth of his touch, the way his mouth had claimed hers as though he'd been starving for her. And for a fleeting moment, her lips curled into a real smile.

Lord Rutherford's narrowed eyes didn't miss it. "Something amusing, my lady?"

Yes, she thought. You. The perfect peacock my parents so desperately want for me.

But what she said was, "Nothing at all, my lord."

Because while her parents already believed she stood beside her perfect match, Lucy's heart was in the stables—burning for the man one hundred times better than this buffoon.

"Do you have someone in mind for yourself?" Margot asked, her voice laced with curiosity as Lucy sprawled across her cousin's bed.

Lucy exhaled slowly. She had finally escaped her mother's exhausting parade of guests and mindless chatter, but her thoughts hadn't quieted. Her mind was still tangled in him—the feel of his hands on her waist, the burn of his kiss still lingering on her lips.

For years, she had silenced that dangerous voice, insisting they were meant for each other. But after today, the voice no longer whispered. It screamed.

She should tell Margot. She wanted to. Her cousin was the only person she trusted with the truth. But admitting to infatuation with a lord was one thing—this was something else entirely.

Instead, Lucy had turned the conversation to Margot's scandalous escapades—confirming what she'd long suspected. Her cousin was no innocent.

Margot's feelings for a certain gentleman still clung stubbornly to her heart. But before Lucy could press her for details, Margot turned the conversation back on her.

"Perhaps," Lucy said, her voice unsteady.

Margot's eyes widened. "Luce," she gasped, practically bouncing beside her. "Who is he? Have I met him?"

Lucy's pulse raced. If she couldn't even convince Margot she wasn't mad for considering…she wasn't even certain yet what she was considering.

"I… well…"

Margot's eager squeal cut her off as she grabbed Lucy's arm. "Oh, you must tell me."

Lucy drew a shaky breath. "You haven't met him."

Margot grinned. "Intriguing. And will he be here at Ashburn Manor this week?"

Would he ever. "Yes."

"Oh, this is thrilling!" Margot clasped her hands together, eyes gleaming. "Does he fancy you as well? Oh, I know he must! You're beautiful, charming, and the daughter of a duke. Your parents will be thrilled. This is positively romantic."

Lucy let her words tumble out before she lost her nerve. "Margot, it's not that simple."

Margot stilled, her smile dimming. "Even more intriguing. Just tell me."

Lucy sat up, hugging her knees to her chest. "He's a servant," she said softly. "In my father's stables."

Silence.

Lucy squeezed her eyes shut. "I take it you don't approve?"

Margot's hand found her arm, warm and steady. "You always have my support," she said gently. "I'm just…

surprised." A pause. Then, with a wicked smile, "Have you... did you...?" She arched her brow. "Is that why you were asking me about—"

"No," Lucy cut in. Though the thought alone made her pulse quicken. Not yet. Her dreams had been filled with such thoughts, and after that kiss... God, she wanted more.

Margot's brow lifted higher. "But you're thinking about it."

Lucy groaned, pressing her fingers to her temples. "I don't know what I'm thinking. We just kissed today." She swallowed hard. "Well... I kissed him, then begged him to kiss me again." Her cheeks heated. "My head's a mess. My body's worse."

Margot smirked. "I knew there was a part of you dying to break free from all of this." Then, with a grin that could only mean trouble, she asked, "And? How was it?"

Lucy closed her eyes, savoring the memory. Perfect. Nothing short of perfect. "Amazing," she whispered.

Margot sighed dreamily. "You have time to figure things out," she said, then her smile faltered, her gaze sharpening. "Rutherford."

Nodding, Lucy's throat tightened. Tears threatened to spill. "What am I going to do? I can't marry Rutherford—not after that kiss. Not when I know what it's supposed to feel like."

Margot studied her for a long moment, then took her hand, her grip warm and steady. "Then you must pursue him."

Lucy blinked. "But… what does that even mean?"

"But… what does that even mean?"

"Spend more time with him. Find out how he feels—be certain of what you want." Margot's lips curved. "And if that means taking him to your bed… Well, that's your choice, too."

Lucy's stomach flipped. "Isn't that… too forward?"

Margot laughed softly, her eyes gleaming with mischief. "The usual rules of courtship no longer apply."

"I suppose," Lucy replied, pondering her cousin's words.

"I love you, Luce," Margot said firmly. "And you deserve to be happy. Figure out what you want—and take it. And if you need help sneaking off to do so, I will help you. Aunt Gem would as well. She'd love to see the look on your parent's faces."

Lucy let out a breathless laugh. "Even if I…" she faltered, swallowing hard. "Even if I decide to… be with him. In that way… before we're married."

Margot's lips curved in a knowing smile. "Even then." But her grin sobered. "Are you aware of how to prevent becoming with child?"

"I am. Sarah told me all about it," Lucy replied.

"Then my last piece of advice is to be certain. Be sure you know your mind and heart."

That was the problem.

She was certain. Certain she was already lost to him. Certain her heart, mind, and body all belonged to the man in her father's stables.

What she didn't know was if he felt the same.

But Margot was right. She had to find out, even if it might destroy her.

That night.

Chapter 3

Clive

Long after dark, Clive Jones was alone that evening in the stables. There, he had the silence to process the torment of his thoughts. And, more importantly, avoid the eager maids who fought for his attention.

He preferred his quiet nights alone. Here, he could dream. For a few fleeting moments, he wasn't just a man in service—he was a man hellbent on building something of his own. A man who might one day own a home, a business. And a man that was far too tempted to risk it all over a single kiss.

Because no matter how hard he tried, his mind kept circling back to her.

His brush moved over the horse's coat in slow, steady strokes, a poor attempt to calm the storm inside him. But it was no use. His body still burned from the memory of her—her lips, soft and seeking, her warmth pressed against him, the way she had begged him to kiss her again.

Fool. He gritted his teeth and climbed the narrow stairs to his loft.

Stripping off his sweat-dampened shirt, he sank onto the edge of his bed, dropping his head into his hands. Cool night air ghosted over his bare skin, but it did nothing to extinguish the fire raging inside him.

Did she lie in bed now, her thoughts consumed with him as his were with her? Or was she entertaining some lord—a man with wealth, power, and a future that matched hers? That thought clenched in his gut, even if he knew the latter was the most probable, and for the best.

He had spent years clawing his way out of nothing, scraping together every coin, chasing every opportunity to carve out a life of his own. And he was close. So damn close.

But no sum of money could ever make him a man worthy of her.

Yet still… he wanted her. Had wanted her since the day they'd met. Two years of swallowing down every look, every stolen moment, every flicker of hope. Two years pretending his heart wasn't already hers.

If her father knew, Clive would be ruined. If not dead. A man like the duke wouldn't just see him sacked. The man had the power to do whatever he wished to him.

But when Lucy had whispered her desire for freedom… he'd felt her pain like a blade to his chest. He knew that longing. Hers was a cage built from duty and expectation. His was the curse of his birth. She wanted freedom from her world. He wanted freedom to build a life of his own.

He ran a hand down his face, willing the ache in his chest to ease. His path had never been easy. He never knew his own father. Just that his surname was Clive, and he was some wealthy merchant who wanted nothing to do with them.

His mother hardly made enough to keep a roof over their head as a barmaid at the local inn, let alone food on their own table. So he'd had to work taking whatever odd job he could from the age of eight years old. He remembered the gnawing ache of an empty belly, and the sting of whispered taunts from other children, branding him a bastard, unwanted and unworthy.

But it was his mother's love that had sustained him, her fierce determination that he would rise above the circumstances of his birth, that he would forge a better life through the strength of his own two hands. He knew from an early age that he must make his own way, catching onto tasks quickly and strong enough as a young lad to do the work of a grown man.

Now, at eight-and-twenty, he was close. He'd learned to live with very little, saving every coin for the future he'd longed for. But no matter how close he was to securing that dream, the one thing he couldn't silence was his yearning for her.

Lady Lucy—with those piercing blue eyes and a laugh that sparkled like the champagne he'd never tasted. No amount of saving or hard work would ever make him a man who could have her.

Yet still, she haunted him.

The memory of their kiss, warm and passionate, sent a shiver down his spine. The feel of her lush body against his, the scent of lavender that clung to her skin... teasing him with the promise of something forbidden and out of reach.

He crossed to his washbasin and splashed cool water over his face, but it did nothing to cool the fire licking beneath his skin—the memory of her kiss, her softness beneath his hands, the scent of lavender that clung to her skin.

Frustrated, he rose again, crossing to his washbasin. He splashed cool water over his face. Tomorrow, he'd bathe in the nearby stream. A treat for his tired muscles. And a cool bath was becoming far more necessary, given the way his body had responded to the duke's daughter.

The rustle of hooves stirred below, followed by something that didn't belong—footsteps.

He moved to investigate, climbing down the stairs. And there he saw her. He stilled, every muscle taut. Moonlight spilled in through the stable doors, casting her in a silver glow, turning her skin to porcelain and her brown hair to a golden color. His breath locked in his throat.

"My lady," he managed, his voice rough with surprise and something dangerous. "You shouldn't be here."

"I needed to see you." Her voice was unsteady. Her gaze dipped to his bare chest, and she faltered. "I…"

Clive swallowed hard, suddenly aware of his state of undress.

"I needed to know," she whispered.

His heart pounded, something raw and reckless twisting inside him. "I'm not sure what you mean."

"I can't stop thinking about you," she confessed, voice barely audible. "When I'm near you. When I'm not." Her gaze softened, something vulnerable breaking through her usual composure. "I need to know if you feel the same."

Clive's chest tightened like a fist.

God help him, yes. He felt it every hour of every day. Every time her voice drifted across the stables. Every time her laughter rang out like a melody meant just for him.

But this—this—was impossible.

Chapter 4

Clive

Clive closed his eyes. Her words—words that should have filled him with joy—pierced like needles. It scarcely mattered what he felt when he wasn't good enough for her.

"Lady Lucy..."

"Lucy," she corrected softly.

His chest tightened. "Lucy," he repeated, knowing he shouldn't address her so intimately. "It doesn't matter. Your place is to wed whomever your parents deem worthy. Mine is to live the life of a working man."

She stepped closer, closing the space between them until they stood mere inches apart. He should step back. God, he should. But his feet refused to move.

"I have little interest in what others say about my place."

Her hand lifted—delicate fingers pressing against his bare chest. His skin heated beneath her palm, and she must have felt the thunder of his heart. He stared at her face, at those sapphire eyes burning bright with defiance.

"Jones…" she breathed.

"Clive," he corrected before he could stop himself. His hand lifted, unable to stop himself, fingers tracing the soft curve of her cheek. "My name is Clive."

She leaned into his touch, her eyes fluttering closed. A soft, broken sound escaped her—his name whispered like a prayer.

God help him.

He drew back, forcing his hand to fall away. "This is mad. You must go back inside. Your father—"

"I'm done living my life for my father," she said, voice low but fierce.

And then she was in his arms, her body molding to his as if she belonged there. The rest of the world fell away. No dukes, no titles, no impossible divides. Only her. Only this aching, desperate need that consumed him whole.

His hands roamed her back, dragging her closer, as his mouth claimed hers in a searing kiss. He forced himself to slow, to rein in the fire threatening to burn them both—but when she parted her lips, when her tongue met his… control shattered.

The heat of her mouth, the sweet taste of her—it devoured his good sense. She was everything forbidden, everything he craved, and he knew one kiss would never be enough.

Her fingers tangled in his hair, nails scraping his scalp as she arched closer, a soft moan spilling from her throat.

The sound shot straight to his cock, hard and aching against her. Desperation clawed at him, but he tempered the kiss, drawing it out into a slow burn that left them both trembling in their embrace.

"Clive," she sighed, breathless and wanting. "Please…"

That single word held a world of longing, of need that echoed his own. But through the haze of desire, a tiny thread of reason persisted. He drew back slightly, just far enough to meet her gaze, his breath mingling with hers. "Lucy, this is wrong. You know that, don't you?"

Her gaze, wicked and mischievous, held his. "I know nothing of the sort." Her hands framed his face, thumbs brushing his jaw. "I want you, Clive. Only you. I have for quite some time."

The last threads of his resistance snapped. With a low growl, he claimed her mouth again, the kiss deep and demanding. A brand of possession. She yielded to him readily, eagerly, her body pliant and responsive in his arms.

Lost in sensation, he scarcely registered their movement, and he'd backed her into the shadows until Lucy's back met the stable wall.

"Clive." Her plea was a husky whisper, laced with urgency. "I need something."

"You don't know what you ask," he ground out.

"I assure you I am quite aware of what I require." Lucy clutched her skirts with one hand, lifting them to expose her thighs. Grasping his wrist, she guided his hand between her legs, pressing him against her heat.

Powerless to deny her, and to his own desperate desire, he let his fingers dance along the sensitive flesh at her opening. When she released a series of low moans, he nearly came undone. "Clive," she moaned.

He let his fingers run lower, teasing her damp folds until they were sheathed inside, a single finger sliding inside of her tight cunt.

"You are so wet, Lucy." He suddenly turned possessive. The idea of another touching her nagged at him. "Has anyone ever touched you here?"

She moaned when he hooked his finger, reaching where he knew would drive her mad.

"Just myself," she said, panting.

The thought of her lying in her bed chamber touching herself almost made him finish in his breeches.

He pressed his body harder against hers, knowing it was wrong, but unable to stop. His covered cock rubbed against her hip while he continued to finger her.

Clive drew a deep breath when she ran her hands along his bare chest, her soft, warm fingertips dancing across his skin and settling in the hair on his chest.

Rocking his hips against hers so he teased his cock through the fabric of their clothing, his body caging hers as his fingers plunged deeper. His thumb circled her pearl, and her moans turned ragged.

"Clive…" Her voice broke, her hips rocking in time with his hand.

He pulled back. "You deserve better than this," he ground out. "Better than me. Better than a bloody stable wall."

"I want you," she panted, clasping him tighter.

His lips claimed hers again, swallowing her cries as he thrust his fingers deeper, coaxing her higher, tighter—until her body locked against his, and she came undone in his arms, shuddering and gasping.

He stilled, watching her fall apart, memorizing the way she looked—lips parted, eyes heavy-lidded, her body limp and sated against his. He had never wanted anything more in his life.

She moaned his name over and over as she rode each wave of her orgasm. Rocking against her one last time, he released in his breeches. Moaning her name against her neck, his climax was more exquisite and intense than anything he'd ever felt before.

They both struggled to catch their breath as they embraced each other, his chest thundering against her in the stillness that followed their storm of passion.

"That," she whispered, voice drowsy and content, "was even better than I imagined." A pause. Then, teasingly, "My cousin was right."

Clive blinked. "Your cousin?"

He lowered her skirts to cover her legs.

"She encouraged me to come tonight." Her smile faded as her fingers brushed his face. "What now? What does this mean for us?"

He stiffened. Reality, cold and cruel, dousing him like icy water.

"I don't know," he admitted, his voice hoarse. "I wish I had an answer. But I don't see a path that leads to happiness for us."

Her face fell. "But you'll try, won't you? Or was this..." Her voice trembled. "Was this just a moment of convenient pleasure for you?"

He cupped her face, holding her gaze. "I don't think I could stay away from you if I tried."

He should, but he didn't think he could. That didn't mean that they had a future beyond him torturing himself for the rest of his life.

Relief flooded her features, and she clung tighter to him. "Then we'll find a way."

If only it were that simple. Clive's hands framed her face. He wished he were as optimistic as she was. She didn't understand.

"You should go," he said softly, brushing a kiss to her temple. "If they find you here..."

"I know," she whispered.

He ached to pull her back into his arms, to lose himself in her sweetness, but the weight of their reality held him back.

She placed a quick kiss on his lips. "I'll return when I can."

"Don't take risks, Lucy. This is dangerous."

"So is a life of discontent," she said, giving his hand a quick squeeze before disappearing into the night.

Clive stood frozen, staring at the empty space she'd left behind, her scent still clinging to his skin. His body still ached with longing. He didn't just want her—he knew her now. Her kiss, her scent, her sighs. He knew what it felt like to hold her, to make her unravel in his arms.

There was no going back now. The carefully drawn lines between them had vanished.

He didn't dare to believe that they could have a life together in truth. The daughter of a duke didn't marry a stable groom, even in fairytales. But however long they might have, he would cherish what he could. He'd record every touch and taste to memory to keep him warm on lonely nights when they both accepted their respective lots in life.

A few stolen moments with her would have to last him for the rest of his life. Because there was no way he could ever experience the same feelings for another.

He was lost. Irrevocably hers.

And the knowledge left him utterly—and royally—fucked.

Chapter 5

Lucy

Lucy gripped her mallet tightly, doing her best to appear at least somewhat interested in the game of Pall Mall. Not because she wanted to—she hated the insipid game—but because her mother had practically shoved her into Lord Rutherford's grasp and insisted she play.

The fake smiles. The dull chatter. The endless fawning over Rutherford's predictable charm—it was all exhausting.

Her mind kept drifting to Clive. His name suited him—strong, grounded—and she loved the way it had felt on her lips. How it still lingered in her thoughts as she imagined his kiss, his touch, his body pressed to hers. She still couldn't believe she'd taken Margot's advice and gone to him.

The sharp clink of mallet striking wood snapped her back to reality. Rutherford's ball sailed neatly through the wicket. He grinned smugly and motioned for Lucy to take her turn.

She barely cared. Gripping her mallet, she swung aimlessly. The ball shot off course, disappearing into the trees.

Rutherford's expression soured as he realized he'd be expected to retrieve it.

"I'll fetch it," Lucy said quickly. "I saw where it went."

He looked as if he might argue, then shrugged and turned back to the other players. Lucy bolted for the trees, eager for even a few minutes of escape.

Scanning the ground for her ball, movement near the stream caught her eye.

Clive.

He emerged from the water, droplets clinging to his bare chest, tracing every hard line of muscle. Sunlight kissed his damp skin, making each curve of his body gleam. He raked a hand through his hair, biceps flexing, and her breath caught.

Dear God… He was magnificent. A Greek god would have paled in comparison.

A faint sigh from somewhere nearby broke her trance. She turned to find a cluster of maids gathered at the edge of the trees, whispering and giggling. They practically devoured him with their eyes. And to her dismay, Sarah was among them.

Jealousy ignited inside her, sharp and scalding. The way they stared—like he was theirs for the taking—made her stomach twist.

Did he welcome their attention? Did he smile at them the way he had smiled at her?

A sudden urge seized her—to storm down to the water, to wrap her arms around him and make it clear that he was hers. She lifted her foot, ready to follow that wild impulse, but Rutherford's voice rang out behind her.

"Lady Lucy!"

Cursing under her breath, she turned back toward the clearing. Spotting her ball just a few steps away, she snatched it up and hurried back.

"What took you so long?" Rutherford asked, irritation sharpening his tone.

"I was searching for my ball," she said sweetly, holding it up as proof. "But I found it."

He appeared to believe her, and not suspect that her naked lover had her in a chokehold. "It has long been your turn."

She set her ball down near where it had exited the game field and quickly took a swing, sending the ball soaring near the wicket.

Lord Rutherford leaned in, his proximity far too familiar, as he murmured something undoubtedly meant to charm. Lucy barely heard him. Her attention had already strayed to the tree line. Was Clive still in the stream? Had he noticed the maids gawking? Was Sarah's advice to embrace her place in society only because she had wanted Clive for herself? The thought sent a sharp pang of irritation through her.

"...wouldn't you agree, Lady Lucy?"

Rutherford's voice yanked her back. She hadn't the faintest idea what he'd said.

"Oh, indeed," she murmured, plastering on her most practiced smile. He puffed up at her approval.

The game dragged on, but her mind never settled. She needed to see Clive—to know what they were, what he wanted.

They'd made no promises. He was free to do as he pleased. But after what had passed between them... surely it had meant something.

She could almost feel his hands sliding over her skin. The way his mouth had claimed hers, desperate yet tender. Her body still hummed with the memory of him.

And those maids... had they felt that too? Had they touched him, kissed him... loved him?

"I believe it's your turn, Lady Lucy. Again." A thread of impatience was obvious in Lord Rutherford's prompt.

Flushed from her wool-gathering, Lucy quickly took her swing. Lord Rutherford eyed her curiously, but then another guest cried out in victory when they finally lobbed their ball through the final wicket. A beautiful sound that the torturous game was over.

"Lord Rutherford," Lucy said, layering her tone with sweetness. "Shall we join the others on the terrace?"

He agreed. Once they reached the terrace, Lucy motioned to a table where Lady Augusta and her Aunt Gem sat. Lord Rutherford pulled out a chair for Lucy and then departed to fetch their drinks.

"Did you have an enjoyable game?" Lady Augusta asked. Lucy had grown quite fond of the matron during various events.

"Indeed," Lucy replied, her mind racing, thoughts of when she'd see Clive again.

"I dare say your smile doesn't quite reach those lovely sapphire eyes of yours," Lady Augusta said, and her Aunt Gem cast Lucy a curious glance.

She couldn't allow others to see through her mask. The last thing she needed was to be pulled aside for another lecture from her mother for failing to play her part. "I assure you, I'm quite well."

Aunt Gem laughed. "Come now, child. Does the reason for your less than jovial mood happen to be tall, blond, and currently staring at you sinfully over his excessive pour of brandy?"

Lucy followed her gaze over to where Rutherford stood with another gentleman, casting her a heated glance over the rim of his glass as he brought it to his lips. The expression grated on her every nerve, and she fought an audible groan.

"Perhaps," Lucy replied, sighing.

"Not that you asked," Lady Augusta started, "but take it from me, my girl. Don't settle for less than you deserve. Happiness is too great a price to pay for someone else's expectations and approval."

"Hear, hear!" Aunt Gem said. Her aunt never had much regard for the rules.

"But the consequences..." Lucy replied, still concerned that Clive might toy with her heart.

Lady Augusta's eyes softened. "There are consequences for all things, my dear. The question is, which one's can you live with?"

That was the million-pound question.

And she must see Clive. Her stomach twisted with urgency. She wouldn't find peace until she knew what he was about.

She saw Rutherford approaching, now also holding a glass of ratafia. He set the glass down in front of her and lowered himself into the seat beside hers. Lucy didn't bother to pretend to drink the ratafia, as what she needed was an escape.

Lucy scanned the terrace. Margot! She stared at her until she finally caught her cousin's gaze, casting her a tight, pleading expression.

Lucy darted her eyes to Rutherford and back to Margot, attempting to communicate what she required. Margot's brow furrowed, and then her eyes widened and gave Lucy a small nod of understanding. She then selected a glass of ratafia from a passing footman.

Margot moved across the terrace to join them, and as soon as she approached the table, she tripped, and her drink spilled all over Lord Rutherford.

"My lord, I am so dreadfully sorry! How clumsy of me," Margot said, seemingly now stable on her feet. "I do hope you will forgive me," she cast an overly sweet smile that almost made Lucy chuckle.

Augusta and Aunt Gem watched the scene curiously, fighting amused expressions, as a footman attempted to help dry Rutherford's coat. Margot's lips curled into a sly smile directed at Lucy when Lord Rutherford huffed.

His face had turned red, and he appeared as if he might scold Margot, who just batted her eyelashes. He drew a deep breath and controlled his features. "Accidents will happen, my lady," he replied. "I must see to my appearance, if you all shall excuse me."

Rutherford didn't actually wait for them to agree before he rose and stomped off toward the entrance to the house.

"Go," Margot whispered. "While you can. I'll cover for you."

Lucy glanced at the older women, who both appeared to puzzle out the situation.

"Sounds like you better go while you can," Lady Augusta said, giving her a knowing look.

Lucy didn't have time to explain, so she darted away, slipping down the terrace stairs. Sprinting along the side of the house, she hurried to the stables. Clive was leading a horse back inside as she approached, fighting to catch her breath.

"Clive," she whispered, breathless.

His gaze flicked to the other stable hands, still working nearby. He jerked his head toward the far side of the stables, silently telling her to wait.

Heart hammering, she obeyed. Minutes stretched like hours until he finally appeared.

"What are you doing here?" he asked, voice low as he pulled her behind the storage shed.

She stared up at him, her breath catching. His shirt clung to his chest, still damp from the stream. Stray droplets glistened on his collarbone, and a lock of hair had fallen across his brow. But it was his eyes—those piercing green eyes—that held her captive.

"I had to see you," she whispered. But then… those maids. The memory curdled inside her, twisting her stomach. She stepped back. "I need to know… are there others? Besides me?"

And she steadied herself, preparing her heart for how he would reply.

Chapter 6

Clive

Clive stared at her, stunned. "Others?" His brow furrowed. "What the devil are you talking about?"

"Women," Lucy said, frustration sharpening her tone. "Are you involved with other women? The maids, perhaps?"

"Of course not," he said firmly. "What kind of man do you take me for?" His pulse pounded. He'd spent two years wanting only her—turning away all others because hers was the face that consumed his thoughts.

Lucy sighed, regret softening her features. "I saw you today. At the stream. There were maids… ogling you."

"I didn't even notice them," he said truthfully.

"So you're not… encouraging their attention?" Her voice wavered. "Or giving them hope that you… might fancy them?"

Clive caught her hand and pulled her close, her body pressing into his. "I know some of them are interested," he said. "But I've never encouraged it. The opposite, in fact. That's part of why I sleep in the stables, far away from the servants' quarters."

Lucy's body relaxed as she melted against him. Her hands splayed over his chest, stilling over the wild, unsteady thrum of his heart, which beat only for her.

He traced a fingertip beneath her chin, lifting her face to his. His voice was rough. "I swear to you, Lucy. In all my time here… you're the only one I've kissed. The only one I've wanted."

"Kiss me," she whispered, her breath shaky. She rose on her toes, her lips grazing his. "Please... I need you."

A groan tore from Clive's throat as he crushed her to him, kissing her with a fierce tenderness that stole his breath. He knew the risk—anyone could find them—but he couldn't stop. Not when she trembled in his arms, not when she clung to him like she feared letting go.

Yet he was the one to pull away, his chest heaving. "Lucy," he rasped. "Someone might see us."

"Perhaps it would be better if they did."

"You can't mean that." He stepped back, forcing space between them. "The consequences..."

"Of course I mean it." She grabbed his hands. "I know my mind, and I know in my heart that this is real."

This was pure torture. "You know nothing about my past," he said. "You were raised in comfort, so you don't understand what our life would be like."

"I may be the daughter of a duke," she shot back, "but I'm not blind to the world."

Clive dragged a hand down his face, fighting the ache that tore through him. "I'm a bastard, Lucy. The unwanted son of a man who discarded me and a mother who..." His voice caught. "My mother sold her body just to keep us alive. And even that wasn't enough. I grew up with nothing—as nothing. I have no name, no fortune, no security. Only a life of struggle, and that's not the life you deserve."

Tears welled in her eyes, and he hated himself for putting them there. But she needed to understand—sometimes love wasn't enough.

Lucy drew a slow, shaky breath. "My father intends to buy me a husband—Lord Rutherford." Her voice cracked with bitter disgust. "That's what a dowry is, isn't it? Payment. A transaction among men." She gave a hollow laugh, her gaze hardening. "I'm no different from a prize mare—a belonging. A means to produce an heir and manage his house."

"Lucy…" He reached for her, but she lifted a trembling hand to stop him.

"Your mother fought with everything she had to give her child a life. You think your mother's struggle meant nothing?" she demanded. "It put you, a wonderful man, on this earth."

Tears shimmered in her eyes, and the sight ripped his heart to pieces.

"Tell me, Clive—do you honestly believe that a life spent beneath a man I despise is a better fate? His to use in whatever way he sees fit. That it's any loss to trade for a life with you?"

His gut twisted at the image—Lucy, married to Rutherford. Forced to endure his touch. The thought of that man taking her to bed... Clive's fists clenched, rage boiling inside him.

"Don't you see?" she whispered, voice breaking. "You offer me something I believed to be mere fantasy—Love. Freedom. A chance to live life on my own terms."

Then she was in his arms, clinging to him like he was her last breath. "I don't care what you can't give me," she said fiercely. "I care far more for the things you can. And I want you. Only you."

"Lucy…" His voice shook. "You deserve more than a life of scraping by. You deserve the entire world—a life untouched by struggle, by fear, by sacrifice. More than what I can offer."

Her eyes flashed with fury. "Are you not hearing me?" She cupped his face, her touch fierce and tender. "I would trade a thousand estates—a thousand empty comforts—for you. Don't you understand?"

She kissed him then—wild and determined—and Clive was lost. He dragged her against him, kissing her deeply, claiming her like she was already his. His hands slid down her back, cupping her bottom as he pulled her flush against his body. She gasped when his fingers skimmed her breast, her soft moan making his blood burn. Palming and squeezing the flesh through her dress while she undulated against him.

"Lady Lucy?"

Clive froze, tearing himself from her as if he'd been scalded. Sarah.

The maid's expression flickered between shock and simmering irritation—tinged with something colder, something possessive. He knew that look. She had been one of the most insistent in pursuing him—and she'd never forgiven his rejection.

"Sarah, I... I can explain," Lucy stammered.

"Lady Lucy," Sarah cut in tightly. "What are you doing out here… again?"

"Please," Lucy pleaded, gripping his hand tighter. "You mustn't tell anyone. I'm begging you."

Sarah's gaze hardened. For a moment, Clive thought she might refuse. But then her shoulders slumped. "I'll keep your secret," she said stiffly. "But this can't happen again."

Lucy's relief flooded her features. "Thank you, Sarah. Truly."

Sarah didn't answer—she simply turned and walked away.

Clive exhaled slowly, reaching for Lucy's hand and gripping it hard. Knowing that when he had to let go, it would break him. "We can't keep risking this," he breathed.

"I know." She stepped closer to him. "But I won't give you up."

He closed his eyes, pressing his forehead to hers. "God help me," he whispered, "neither will I."

Chapter 7

Lucy

That evening, Lucy stared blankly out the dining room window, the low hum of conversation washing over her like dull background noise. The table gleamed with crystal and silver, her mother's flawless attempt to impress their guests. Every detail had been planned to perfection.

And yet, to Lucy, it all felt suffocating.

She sat beside Lord Rutherford, a fixed smile plastered to her face as she nodded along to his endless monologue—something about a hunting exploit, or perhaps his estates. She hadn't caught much beyond the self-congratulation in his tone. Her mind was elsewhere—lost in thoughts of Clive.

God, she couldn't stop thinking about him. Since Sarah had caught them in the stables, she knew their fragile secret was on borrowed time. How much longer before word reached her parents? Before her world—and his—came crashing down?

"Wouldn't you agree, Lady Lucy?" Rutherford's sharp tone cut through her thoughts.

She blinked, scrambling to recall what he'd just said. "Oh, yes," she murmured hastily. "Quite."

He preened, chest puffed out like a strutting peacock. "I knew you'd see it my way. A lady of your discernment could hardly do otherwise."

Lucy's smile tightened until her cheeks ached. Fool. He hadn't the faintest idea how deeply she loathed him. How desperately she yearned to be anywhere but here.

But why should he suspect otherwise? She'd played her part to perfection—the dutiful daughter, the poised young lady. No one, least of all Rutherford, would ever guess that beneath her prim exterior burned a wild, aching desire to cast propriety aside and run to Clive.

The memory of the stables crept back to her—Clive's kiss, fierce and consuming, the strength of his arms as he held her close. She could still feel his breath on her skin, still taste the faint trace of salt on his lips.

"Lady Lucy?" Rutherford's voice dragged her back again, sharper this time. "Are you well? You look a bit flushed."

She dabbed her cheeks with her napkin, willing the heat in her face to fade. "I'm fine," she lied. "It must be the wine."

He seemed satisfied with the excuse—not that he truly cared. Without missing a beat, he resumed his tiresome discourse. Something about his properties. Or perhaps his dogs. She hardly knew. She hardly cared.

When the meal finally ended, Lucy slipped away the moment the ladies retreated to the drawing room. She scanned the room for Margot, hoping to thank her for her help earlier, but Lady Augusta caught her eye and waved her over.

"That was quite the performance your cousin put on this afternoon," Lady Augusta murmured, her tone laced with dry amusement.

"I don't know what you mean," Lucy said, though her weak smile faltered beneath Lady Augusta's knowing look.

"I think you do." Augusta's gaze sharpened. "You have the look of a woman in love… and I know it isn't with that buffoon Rutherford."

Lucy's breath caught. Love? Was that what this was? She'd told herself she didn't know what she felt—that her heart was still sorting through the confusion and chaos of wanting Clive. But hadn't she already decided she'd risk everything for him?

"I'm still figuring out what I feel," she admitted softly.

Lady Augusta stepped closer, her expression gentler. "He's a servant, isn't he?"

Panic flared in Lucy's chest. She glanced around the room, desperate to be sure no one had overheard. "I…"

"I mean no judgment," Augusta said quietly. "But if this were a guest of your mother's choosing, you wouldn't be sneaking off like a thief in the night."

Lucy exhaled, her shoulders sagging beneath the weight of her secret. The words spilled from her lips before she could stop them. "He works in the stables."

Augusta's brow lifted, but her expression remained kind. "I won't tell a soul," she promised, giving Lucy's hand a reassuring squeeze. "You can't help who you love. Just make certain you know his heart, and that you're sure of his character."

Lucy nodded, but her stomach twisted with uncertainty. She believed Clive cared for her. He'd said as much. Yet doubt gnawed at her. Had their passion clouded her judgment? Had she mistaken his desire for love?

And she must know what it was he felt before setting her entire life on fire for him.

Chapter 8

CLIVE

The next day, Clive shoveled straw from the stalls, lost in thought. He barely noticed the ache in his muscles, too consumed by the face he couldn't shake from his mind.

He'd spent half the night counting and recounting his savings. It was nearly enough to rent a small cottage in the country—a modest home where he might start a breeding business. But would it be enough to give her the life she deserved? Could he risk everything, knowing she might be leaving behind comfort, wealth, and security?

"There you are," a flirtatious voice purred from behind him.

Clive turned, muscles tensing. Lucy's maid stood before him, her smile far too familiar.

"Did you need something?" He took a step back.

"Absolutely, Handsome." She advanced, swaying her hips. "And I can give you exactly what you need as well."

"You've nothing I want," he said flatly. He kept his tone firm. Cruel, even. There could be no misunderstanding. There was only one woman he needed.

The maid laughed. "You think you'll get your hands on some of that duke's fortune if you charm his daughter?"

Clive's jaw clenched. "No. I only want her."

The faster she departed, the better. He didn't want anyone to see him with Lucy's maid and get the wrong idea. Servants talk. A lot.

"You could have us both," she said darkly. "Especially if you want me to keep quiet about what I know."

Clive stiffened. "You already promised."

She stepped closer, forcing him back until his spine met the stable wall. "There are plenty of ways you could silence me."

Before he could push her away, movement near the stable doors caught his eye.

Lucy.

She stood frozen, hurt darkening her sapphire eyes.

"Lucy," Clive called, voice low with panic.

Sarah turned around, barely masking her smug smile. "We'll finish this later," she said sweetly over her shoulder, sauntering past Lucy without a trace of shame.

"Lucy, please, allow me to—"

"Mister Jones," Lucy interrupted, her voice clipped and formal. "I require my horse to be saddled. Immediately."

The cold sliced through his heart. "Of course," he managed. "But if I could just explain—"

A shadow appeared at the entrance—a well-dressed older woman watching them with quiet curiosity.

"There's nothing to explain," Lucy said stiffly, her gaze flicking to the newcomer. "All I require is my horse."

Clive's hands trembled as he reached for the nearest saddle. "Please, Lucy," he whispered, abandoning formality in his desperation. "It's not what you think."

Lucy's expression didn't falter, but a muscle twitched in her jaw. "What I think, Mister Jones," she said, voice like ice, "is that I've been a fool. Now my horse, if you please."

His chest tightened. She didn't believe him. After everything… she didn't believe him.

He walked her horse to the mounting block, gripping the reins tightly to steady his shaking hands. The older woman murmured something to Lucy. He caught only fragments. Character… True intentions…

Clive glanced at the other woman, knowing he couldn't speak about the matter in front of her. Instead, he watched helplessly as Lucy mounted Thor with fluid grace, her back ramrod straight. She gathered the reins, her knuckles white with tension.

"Lucy, wait," Clive whispered.

Her sapphire eyes met his, hurt and confusion swirling in their depths. For a heartbeat, her carefully constructed facade cracked, revealing the raw pain beneath. Then, with a sharp click of her tongue, she urged her mount forward, riding away from him.

Clive's chest ached as he watched her go.

"Give her some space, my boy," the older woman said gently.

He spun to face her, fear gripping him that she knew their secret. "I don't know what you mean." His voice came out too fast, too defensive. "The skies look like rain—I only meant to ensure Lady Lucy remained safe."

The woman's gaze didn't waver. "Did you require assistance, my lady?" Clive asked hastily. "A horse, perhaps? Lady…"

"Lady Augusta," she said, stepping closer. "And that won't be necessary. I came here to meet you for myself."

Fear bolted through him. Had Lucy's maid already run to her family? Had this woman come to see him cast off the estate?

"Why me?" he asked warily.

Lady Augusta's lips curved in a knowing smile. "Let us speak plainly," she said. "I've grown fond of Lady Lucy, and I needed to know your intentions."

His heart pounded. "I… I don't know what you mean."

"You love her," Lady Augusta said simply.

Clive swallowed hard, stunned by how easily she'd pierced the truth. His instinct was to deny it—to protect Lucy, to protect himself—but the words wouldn't come.

Instead, he exhaled, voice raw and low. "I love her enough to let her go. Enough to put her happiness above my own."

Lady Augusta's expression softened. "Then you'll need help."

His breath caught. "Help?"

"If you truly mean to build a life with her, you'll need allies." She smiled faintly. "And I'm offering to be one."

Clive stared at her, torn between hope and suspicion. "Why would you help me?"

"Because love is precious," she said. "And if that's what you feel for Lady Lucy, you'll need every advantage you can get to survive her father."

He hesitated, searching her face for deception—but found only warmth.

"I haven't told her yet," he admitted quietly. "That I love her. I am… afraid." He swallowed hard. "I'm not certain what future is even possible."

Suddenly, and unexpectedly, Lady Augusta's eyes flickered with recognition. She reached out, allowing her gloved fingers to brush Clive's cheek in a maternal gesture. "There's something about you, young man. Something familiar that I can't quite place."

"I… I don't know what to say, my lady," he managed. She continued to stare at him, running her thumb on his cheek. Clive shifted on his feet, unsure what to think about the awkward interaction. And he silently willed Lucy not to reappear. He wasn't certain how he'd explain yet another woman with their hands on him.

"You look so much like my son," Lady Augusta finally said. "What was your father's name?"

"I am unsure, my lady," Clive replied, tamping down his own embarrassment related to the truth of his birth. "Jones is my mother's family name, but my mother named me Clive after my father's surname."

Lady Augusta's eyes widened. "Clive," she murmured, continuing to study his face. "Clive Jones." The way she spoke his name was tinged with a hint of remorse.

"What is it, my lady? I don't understand."

She released his cheek and sought his hand, clasping it in hers. "I believe my late husband just might be your father."

"That can't be," he said, his voice barely more than a whisper.

But the look in Lady Augusta's eyes told him she believed it was true. And suddenly, the ground beneath his feet no longer felt steady.

"Impossible..." he murmured, but deep down, something inside him, something he'd buried long ago, rose to the surface. He might learn who his father was.

Chapter 9

Clive

Clive was still reeling from the conversation he'd had with Lady Augusta when a low rumble of thunder broke through his thoughts.

Lucy. His heart stuttered. She was nowhere in sight, and the sky had turned an ominous shade of gray.

Striding purposefully toward the nearest stall, he knew he must go after her. The first fat drops of rain began to fall as Clive swung himself into the saddle. He urged his mount forward. Digging his heels into the horse's sides, he rode hard, leaning low over the animal's neck as they tore across the sodden fields.

Rain lashed against his face, soaking his shirt and stinging his eyes. The wind howled through the trees, dragging branches low across the path.

"Bloody hell," Clive growled, fighting to control his mount as a vicious gust of wind threatened to unseat him.

Lightning split the sky, followed by a roar of thunder, as Clive glimpsed a rider ahead. "Lucy!" he called out, his voice lost in the storm.

Determination surged through him. Clive pressed on, heedless of the danger, focused solely on reaching the woman he loved. The storm raged around them, mirroring the tempest of emotions within his chest.

Clive's heart leaped as he got her closer in his sights. Closing the distance, he rode up alongside Lucy's horse. Her gaze fixed on him, a mixture of surprise and lingering hurt. Huddled beneath a tree, the rain running in rivulets down her face.

"Lucy, please," he called out over the howling wind. "You misunderstood—"

"I don't want to hear it, Clive." Her voice shook, ragged with betrayal. "I believed you. I believed I might actually be enough for you. That you might…" Her voice broke, and she turned away.

Enough? She thought she wasn't enough for him?

He couldn't let her believe that. Without thinking, Clive reached out and grabbed her reins, pulling their horses closer.

"Listen to me," he pleaded. "Your maid… she sought me out. I told her no—a long time ago and again today. There's only one woman who has ever had my heart." His voice dropped low, thick with emotion. "And she's sitting before me now."

Lucy's lips parted in surprise, her eyes wide and searching his. "Clive, I—"

But he couldn't hold back any longer. He reached for her, grasping her waist and pulling her from her saddle into his arms. Her body landed across his lap, rain-soaked and shivering, but he didn't care. His mouth found hers, desperate and consuming, a kiss that poured out everything he felt. His frustration, his fear… and his love.

Lucy froze for only a breath before melting into him, her fingers tangling in his hair as she kissed him back with the same fire. The cool rain was a stark contrast to the heat blazing between them.

When they finally broke apart, Clive cupped her face in his hands. "I love you," he rasped. "I should have told you sooner—yesterday, or hell, months ago. But I won't have you doubting it now."

Thunder cracked above them, the storm raging as fiercely as his emotions. Lucy shivered against him, and protective instinct took over.

"There's a cabin nearby," he said urgently. "We need to get out of this storm before you fall ill."

She nodded, her teeth chattering. "L-lead the way."

Clive helped Lucy seat herself back in her saddle. They rode side by side through the downpour as the horses moved carefully over the slick ground. When the outline of the cabin emerged from the trees, Clive breathed a sigh of relief.

He dismounted quickly, tying the horses under a narrow awning before hurrying around to Lucy. She slid from her saddle into his arms, her soaked gown clinging to her body. He averted his gaze, forcing himself to focus on her safety rather than the way the wet fabric traced every curve.

Inside the cabin, Clive moved swiftly, locating flint and tinder, starting a fire. As warmth filled the space, he turned to Lucy, who stood shivering by the door.

"You need to get out of those wet clothes," he said, his voice rough with concern. "There should be blankets in the bedchamber there."

Lucy's eyes widened, a blush creeping across her cheeks. She departed into the chamber and then returned with a couple of large blankets.

Clive caught the uncertainty in her eyes. "I'll turn my back."

As he turned away, Clive's mind raced. The intimacy of their situation, the memory of their kiss, and the sound of rustling fabric behind him threatened to undo his resolve. He closed his eyes, silently praying for strength to keep his gaze fixed on the wall.

"I'm undressed," she called out to him.

"Does that mean I should continue staring at the wall or that I should turn around?" he asked, trying to keep his tone light.

She laughed, and it sounded like the tinkling of the most perfectly tuned bells. "Turn around. You must get out of those wet clothes, too."

Clive turned slowly. His breath caught at the sight of her—bare shoulders exposed, her body wrapped tightly in a blanket that clung to her curves. The lucky blanket. Stray tendrils of damp hair curled around her face, and her skin glowed in the firelight.

Clive began unfastening buttons on his shirt.

"Should I turn around?" she asked, but her gaze remained fixed on him.

"Every part of me belongs to you, so the choice is yours." He knew he played with fire, but it didn't make it any less true.

He shrugged out of his shirt and hung it on a rack before the fire with her clothing. Then he kicked out of his boots and removed his stockings.

His fingers hovered at the waistband of his breeches. Lucy's eyes never left him, her gaze flicking from his chest to the line of muscle disappearing beneath the damp fabric.

When he pushed his breeches down over his hips, his cock jutted hard and proud.

Lucy gasped, her eyes widening.

"Have you seen a man before?" he asked, his voice low.

She swallowed hard, her gaze still fixed below his waist. "Only you," she whispered.

The words unraveled him. He grabbed the second blanket and hastily wrapped it around his shoulders before temptation drove him too far. His body thrummed with unspent need, but he forced himself to breathe, to calm the storm within him.

"If I have my way," Clive murmured, moving to stand beside her before the fire, "you'll never see another."

He wasn't sure how they'd make that possible. How to defy her family, her station, or the weight of society's expectations. But none of that mattered right now. They would find a way. They had to.

The storm raged on, lightning crackling across the sky and illuminating the room in brief, jagged flashes.

Rain hammered the roof, and thunder growled like an angry beast. Yet inside the cabin, all was quiet—only the crackling fire and the pounding of his heart.

"I love you too," Lucy said softly, shattering the silence.

His breath hitched. "Sweetheart… I don't expect anything from you. I know this is fast, and mad, and—"

"Will you hush?" she teased, turning to face him. Her fingers curled in the blanket at her chest, but her smile softened him. "I love you," she said again, her voice stronger. "I am yours. And no one else matters."

A low groan escaped him as he seized her waist, pulling her closer. He kissed her gently at first, until need overtook him. His lips claimed hers with a desperation that stole his breath, his fingers threading into her damp hair as he deepened the kiss.

Lucy pressed into him, her body warm and pliant beneath the blanket. His slipped from his grasp, tumbling to the floor and leaving him bare before her.

He broke the kiss, chest heaving, and cupped her face in his hands. "We don't have to—"

"I want this," she interrupted, her palm pressed flat against his chest, her fingers tracing the frantic beat of his heart. "I want you. Make me yours."

"Are you certain?" His voice was rough with restraint. Even if being with her was what he wanted most in the world.

Instead of answering, Lucy let her blanket fall away, pooling at her feet. Her bare body stood illuminated in the firelight, soft curves and creamy skin bathed in gold.

"More certain than I've ever been," she said.

"You're perfect," Clive breathed, scooping her into his arms. He would not make love to her for the first time on the floor of the hunting cabin. Perhaps the second or third time, but not the first.

He carried her to the bedchamber and laid her down gently before climbing over her, bracing his weight on his arms as he stared down at her. Clive couldn't take his eyes off of her, memorizing every curve of her body.

"Please, Clive. I need to feel you."

He kissed her jaw, then her throat, moving lower until his lips found the curve of her breast. His mouth closed over her nipple, budded tightly beneath his tongue. Lucy gasped, arching into him, fingers threading through his hair. He tasted a faint hint of lavender on her skin, and it drove him mad as he sucked harder.

"You must enjoy this," he stated, smiling against her skin as he moved to her other breast. He kissed, licked, and sucked until her gasps turned to low, breathless moans.

"You must tell me if I do anything you don't like," he said as he continued to explore her body with his lips and tongue.

"I love all of it so far."

He chuckled darkly. "Then I think you are going to especially enjoy this."

He kissed lower, down the flat plane of her stomach, his fingers tracing the curve of her waist. When he reached her thighs, he gently pushed them apart, baring her dark nest of curls to him.

"Clive…" she whispered, her breath shaky.

"Trust me," he murmured.

And then his mouth was on her. The first flick of his tongue against her pearl made her cry out, her fingers tangling tightly in his hair. He circled the sensitive nub, teasing and tasting until she writhed beneath him.

"Oh God… yes," she moaned. "More. More."

He grinned against her and then let his tongue shift lower until he reached her opening. She was already so wet, and he lapped at the proof of her desire. Lucy was the best thing he'd ever tasted, and he'd drink from her every day if she'd allow him to.

Plunging his tongue inside of her tight opening, she bucked and moved her hips against his face. Withdrawing his tongue, he replaced it with a single finger, sliding it deep inside of her.

"You feel incredible," he rasped. "So warm. So perfect."

"Don't stop," she begged.

He teased her, gliding his finger inside of her cunt. He already imagined how tight she would be wrapped around his cock, a bit of liquid already pooling at the head from the anticipation.

"Come for me, Sweetheart," he urged. "Let me hear you."

Their eyes met, and he didn't look away from her when he flicked his tongue against her nub again while fingering her.

She released a low moan, fighting to keep her eyes open.

"That wasn't nearly loud enough," he said. Instead of a single flick, he pressed his tongue against her pearl and circled it with ample pressure.

Lucy cried out several moans and gripped his head with her hands.

"Much better," he praised.

He licked and sucked. She held his head where she wanted him and moved her hips in pace with his efforts. When he felt her core clench tightly around his finger, his eyes rolled back in his head.

Lucy released a steady stream of loud moans, her body trembling from her orgasm.

Clive withdrew his finger and sucked it into his mouth, needing to taste her climax for himself. He hovered himself back over her, kissing her lips. She immediately opened to him and he massaged her tongue with his, allowing her to taste herself.

His needy cock jutted between them, rubbing against her seam as he kissed her. Her arms wrapped around him, pulling him close. He'd never felt so loved and needed in his life.

"Tell me if I hurt you," he whispered against her lips, as he ran his hand between them to position himself at her opening.

Lucy instinctively wrapped her legs around him, drawing him even closer. "You could never hurt me."

Clive guided himself to her entrance, moving slowly, giving her time to adjust. He pushed inside by inches, his forehead pressed to hers as they breathed together.

He moved with a quick thrust, breaking through her maidenhead and making her wince. "Are you all right?"

She nodded. "Kiss me."

Lowering his lips to hers, he kissed her deeply as he moved inside of her. When he withdrew and re-entered her in a single thrust, her legs gripped his waist tighter as she moaned wildly into their kiss.

"You're mine," Clive groaned, driving into her harder. "Do you hear me?"

"Yes," she gasped, her fingernails biting his skin. "I'm yours."

"Say it again."

"I'm yours," she panted, clutching his shoulders as her hips rocked to meet his. "And you're mine."

"I've been yours since the first time I saw you."

His movements turned frantic, coming more undone from the way her breath quickened and the tight grip she kept on him. Her moans grew louder and louder, and at one point she even bit into the side of his neck. He'd never get enough of being with her.

He slowed his thrusts when her head rolled back and her cunt tightened so hard around him it took all he had to keep from exploding inside of her. Sliding inside of her a few more times, he prolonged her orgasm before she stilled.

Clive quickly withdrew and coated her stomach with steady streams of his seed.

"Don't move," Clive whispered.

Searching the room, he found a clean cloth and returned to Lucy. He gently cleaned the blood from between her legs and the spend he'd left on her stomach. Using the cloth on himself, he cleaned himself and then crawled back beside Lucy, gathering her into his arms. Their bodies fit together perfectly, her head tucked beneath his chin, her fingers idly tracing along his chest.

He pressed a tender kiss to her forehead. "Are you sure you're all right, Sweetheart?"

Lucy tipped her head back to meet his gaze, her sapphire eyes warm and content. "I've never been better."

"Lucy," he said quietly, his fingers trailing along her bare back, "I never dared to believe this could be real."

"And yet here we are," she replied, her lips curving in a soft smile.

The warmth of her body against his should have been enough to soothe him, but a shadow of doubt gnawed at him. "But what happens when we leave this cabin?" His voice thickened with unease. "Your father expects you to marry a man of his choosing. He'll never allow this… us."

Lucy's fingers found his jaw, tracing the strong line as if to erase his worry. "I don't recall you asking me to marry you."

Clive let out a breathless laugh, but his smile faded. "Your father would never allow it."

"Shh," she murmured, pressing a fingertip to his lips. "Let's not think of that now." Her gaze softened. "Tell me… if you could have anything in the world, what would it be?"

Clive's hand covered hers, pressing her palm to his chest. "You," he said without hesitation. "You as my wife. A quiet cottage we could call home. Nothing grand, but ours. Enough land to keep horses so I could raise and breed them. Enough coin to be content… and enough love to fill a lifetime."

"That's exactly the life I want, too." Her voice trembled with longing. "We'll find a way."

Clive's arms tightened around her, his heart thudding beneath her palm. "We must. Because I can't go on without you."

As they lay there, basking in the afterglow of their lovemaking and shared dreams, the weight of the uphill battle they faced settled on Clive's chest.

"We'll devise a plan," Lucy said, her lips brushing against his chest, her voice a determined promise. "If we must run… we'll run. By the end of this wretched house party, we'll have everything figured out."

He pressed a lingering kiss to her temple, breathing her in as if he could etch her scent into his soul. Surely, he thought, it couldn't be as simple as that. She was the daughter of a duke, after all. There would be consequences. Sacrifices.

But whatever it took—whatever price he had to pay—he would pay it.

Because the moment Lucy had given herself to him, he'd made a vow in his heart.

He wouldn't lose her. Not to her father. Not to the likes of Rutherford. Not to anyone.

She was his, and no force in the world would keep him from her now.

Chapter 10

Lucy

The next morning, Lucy's eyes fluttered open, her limbs heavy and deliciously sore from the night before. Memories of the hunting cabin flooded her mind—Clive's touch, his kiss, the way their bodies had moved together, hesitant at first and then wild and unrestrained as the storm raged outside.

An ache bloomed low in her belly, and she pressed her face into the pillow to muffle a moan. Every inch of her felt different—alive—as if she'd only just discovered her own body.

But with that new awareness came an unsettling weight. She'd given herself to the man she loved, a man her parents would never accept. What now? Would they have to run away? When? How?

One thing was certain: she couldn't stay away from Clive. Not now. Not ever.

Once she'd left her bed, Sarah barely spoke to her that morning, aside from muttering something sharp about her late rising. Lucy suspected her maid was still smarting from her failed attempt to seduce Clive. The thought sent heat surging through Lucy's veins—anger and jealousy tangled in her chest.

She nearly confronted Sarah about it, but a sharp rap at the door interrupted her.

"Cousin! What have you been up to?" came Margot's knowing tone when she poked her head inside the door. Without waiting for a response, she breezed into the room in a swirl that was typical of her cousin.

Sarah cast Lucy a suspicious look, clearly eager to hear the answer. After her late return the previous evening, Lucy had claimed she'd caught a chill riding in the rain—an excuse she'd crafted because she couldn't trust her maid with the truth. But it had allowed her to remain in her chamber for the evening.

Lucy forced a tight smile. "That will be all, Sarah."

The maid lingered, casting her an annoyed smile before exiting the room, closing the door behind her. As soon as she was gone, Margot seized Lucy's hand and dragged her to the settee.

"Now," Margot demanded, eyes sparkling. "Tell me everything. Aunt Gem seems convinced you've taken up with a man." She grinned. "I can only assume you've been sneaking out to see your… well, what shall we call him?"

"His name is Clive," Lucy muttered.

"Oh, Clive, is it?" Margot's grin widened. "How delightfully scandalous. Now tell me everything before I die of curiosity."

"I'm trying!" Lucy shot back, laughing despite herself. "But if you keep interrupting, I'll never finish."

Margot clasped her hands dramatically, miming silence.

So Lucy told her. Not every sinful detail, but enough to make Margot's eyes widen and her smile soften. "I love him, Margot," Lucy finished, her voice barely a whisper. "With all my heart. But how can we possibly be together? My father will never allow it."

To Lucy's surprise, Margot's face lit up with excitement. "To hell with what your father wants! You're one-and-twenty, and of legal age. Just leave. Be with him."

Lucy shook her head. "I can't just disappear without telling my parents."

Margot's smile faded, and she gave a thoughtful sigh. "I suppose that isn't the best course. But you should prepare yourself. If you defy the duke, he may demand that you either obey him… or leave for good."

Lucy swallowed hard. "Do you really think my father would cast me out? Is he that cold?"

Margot scoffed. "Have you met him? He barely tolerates me—and I'm only related to him through marriage."

She wasn't wrong. Her father cared more for appearances than for her. Always had. But she knew he did care for her in his own way. "Could he keep Grandmama's inheritance from me?"

"No," Margot said firmly. "That money is yours now that you've come of age. It may take time to gain access to it, but a good solicitor will see to it. He can't keep it from you."

Lucy's thoughts spun. Even with her inheritance, what would she and Clive do in the meantime? How would they survive until they had enough to build their life together?

"If it's money that concerns you," Margot said, as if reading her mind, "Aunt Gem would help. And if not her, I will." She squeezed Lucy's hand. "You'll never be alone. Or on the streets. You know that, don't you?"

Tears stung Lucy's eyes—overwhelmed by gratitude, the weight of her choices, and the unwavering love of her cousin. "Thank you," she choked out. "Truly."

Margot pulled her into a fierce hug. "I'm just glad you've found your match." Then she grinned wickedly. "And it'll be the scandal of the season. Some might expect it from me, but you, Cousin?" She clutched her chest in mock offense. "I am positively green with envy."

Lucy couldn't help but laugh. Trust Margot to find excitement in the threat of social ruin. But oddly enough, it soothed her. Besides, she'd be gone, living a contented life with the man of her dreams.

"When are you going to tell them?" Margot asked.

"I think tomorrow would be best. Mama's masquerade ball is tonight, so she'll already be on edge. Heaven forbid we have a single flower out of place." Lucy made no attempt to temper her sarcasm.

Lucy thought she heard something outside of her door, but then the sound was covered with Margot's laughter.

Margot smirked. "How fun would it be to scatter flower petals across her freshly polished ballroom floor?"

"She'd suffer an apoplexy," Lucy laughed.

The cousins collapsed into each other in a fit of giggles. But as Lucy wiped her eyes, she knew it wasn't over. There was still so much at stake. Her father's wrath. The uncertainty of what her future held.

But that was tomorrow's problem.

"Now," Lucy said with a grin, "I'm certain I'm not the only one sneaking around lately. I want to hear all about your escapades."

Chapter 11

Lucy

Lucy was relieved that her mother had chosen a masquerade theme for the ball. It was much easier to hide behind an actual mask. Although, she should thank the stars that her mother had taken little notice of her since the house party began.

Margot had kept her company for a while as Lucy attempted to avoid Rutherford. But her cousin was currently enjoying a waltz with Lord Steelhaven, and Lucy couldn't help but beam at them as they turned about the floor.

She kept herself hidden near one of the refreshment tables, doing her best to keep anything from dirtying her solid white gown, made from the most expensive fabrics.

Her mother selected it, of course, down to each detail in the cream feather mask she wore. She chuckled to herself at the humor in being presented as an innocent, knowing that just the day prior, she had Clive's head between her thighs.

"My dear Lady Lucy," Rutherford purred, materializing beside her. "You outshine even the stars tonight."

Lucy forced a tight smile. He must have spent all afternoon thinking up that one. "You're too kind, my lord."

"Nonsense," he drawled, offering his arm. "Come, a dance?"

She had no choice but to accept. His hand gripped her waist with more pressure than necessary, his fingers digging into her side as he guided her across the floor.

"You move with such grace," he murmured, his lips far too close to her ear. "I daresay you'd make a fine partner... in more ways than one."

Lucy's stomach churned, but she kept her smile fixed. "I imagine any woman would be fortunate to have such an opportunity." Her gaze swept the room, searching for an escape.

Then she heard it—her father's voice, low and pleased: "... an excellent match. Rutherford's connections..."

The words struck as if she's been slapped. A transaction. That's all this was—a cold, calculated exchange. She really was being treated like a prized pony. Whatever faint hope she'd clung to, that her parents might understand, or come to accept, her love for Clive, was gone.

"Are you all right, my dear?" Rutherford's tone dripped with false concern. "You've gone pale."

"I... I think I'm overheated," Lucy managed, barely able to speak past the lump in her throat. "The room is quite warm."

"I'll fetch you some refreshment," Rutherford said, clearly relishing the chance to play the devoted suitor.

The moment he turned, Lucy exhaled shakily, her thoughts racing. She had no choice now—no hope of convincing her parents. She and Clive would have to run. Soon.

A sudden shift in the crowd caught her eye, and her heart faltered.

A tall figure in midnight blue moved toward her. Even behind the mask, she knew him—her body knew him—before he even spoke.

A sudden ripple in the crowd caught Lucy's attention. Her breath caught as a tall, masked figure in midnight blue approached. Even with his face obscured, Lucy's body responded, recognizing Clive instantly. Her heart raced, palms suddenly damp against her silk gloves.

"May I have this dance, my lady?" Clive's voice was low, barely audible above the music, but it sent electricity radiating throughout her body.

She couldn't speak, could only nod as he led her back onto the floor. His hand settled on her waist, sending heat curling through her.

"You look breathtaking," Clive murmured, his lips brushing her ear.

"Clive," she sighed. "I didn't know you could dance. I mean...sorry."

He grinned at her, even though there was a hint of heartbreak in his eyes. "I take no offense. Through the years, I watched others and memorized the steps."

Her heart twisted painfully. "I'm so glad to see you." I missed you. I need you.

"Please," Clive interrupted, voice tight. "Let me speak, Sweetheart. I fear our time is short."

The sorrow in his voice made her heart clench. "What's wrong?"

His hand pressed just a little tighter at her waist, like he was anchoring her to him. "I love you, Lucy. More than anything. And no matter what happens, I need you to remember that."

"Clive—" Her voice shook.

But before she could ask what he meant, the music swelled to a crescendo. In one swift motion, Clive spun her outward. When she turned back—he was gone.

"Clive?" she called, panic rising. "Clive!"

"My dear Lady Lucy," Rutherford's smug voice intruded. "I've brought you a bit of ratafia."

Lucy barely heard him, her eyes still sweeping the room. "I... I'm not feeling well," she muttered. "Perhaps we could—"

Rutherford seized her hand, his fingers clamping tightly around hers. "Nonsense," he chuckled darkly. "A drink, and then another dance. It will set you right."

He pressed the glass into her hand. The smell turned her stomach. Why did Clive speak as if they might never see each other again?

"Forgive me," Lucy said, wrenching her hand free. "I must retire."

Before Rutherford could protest, she bolted through the crowd, her pulse pounding. She needed to find Clive. Something was wrong.

Lucy made it just outside the ballroom and a familiar voice called to her.

"Lucy, darling," the duchess called. "Where are you off to in such a hurry?"

Lucy froze. Turning slowly, she was met with icy stares from her parents. Of course, they would choose that moment to notice her.

"I was just..." Lucy began, but the words died on her lips as she took in their grim expressions.

"I think," her father said coldly, "it's time we had a conversation about your... indiscretions."

Lucy swallowed hard. Her throat felt tight, her heart thundering. "Father," she managed, her voice barely steady, "allow me to explain—"

"Indeed you shall." His voice was low and dangerous.

Panic twisted in her chest. She had to think—quickly. And she had to find Clive before it was too late.

Chapter 12

Lucy

Lucy braced herself as her parents glared at her.

"Not here," her father hissed. "Come with us. Now."

The Duke's hand clamped around her arm, her mother flanking her other side. They marched her out of the ballroom and down the corridor, little better than a prisoner.

Lucy's heart pounded. How much did they know? What would happen to her? To Clive?

Her father urged her inside his study, the heavy door thudding shut behind them.

"How could you be so foolish?" her mother snapped, her voice trembling with rage. ""Dallying with a servant?

Have you forgotten your place? Thankfully, your maid has more regard for your reputation than you do."

Lucy staggered under the force of her mother's disappointment — and Sarah's betrayal. So it had been her. Of course it had.

"Clive is more than a servant," Lucy shot back, her voice unsteady but firm. "He's—"

"He's nothing," her father growled. "A nobody who will drag you down into the mud with him. After everything we've given you, this is how you repay us? By spreading your legs for a bloody stable hand?"

Lucy's breath caught in her throat, her face burning. "I… I…"

"So you don't deny it," her father sneered. "Well, you won't see him again. You'll marry Rutherford as planned. The arrangements have already been made. And you won't breathe a word of this."

Lucy's mind reeled, her father's words echoing in her ears. Arranged? The injustice of it all burned through her veins like fire.

"No," she whispered, then louder, "No! I won't do it. I love Clive, and I won't be forced into a loveless marriage to play the part you have created for me."

"Oh, Lucy," her mother said, her voice softening into pity. "This isn't love. It's infatuation — rebellion, even. It will pass."

But Lucy knew better. What she felt for Clive was real. Unshakeable and unchangeable.

In a burst of desperation, Lucy wrenched herself free from her mother's grasp, tears stinging her eyes. "I can't—I won't—"

And then she was running, her white gown billowing behind her. Her heart pounded a frantic rhythm in her chest, fear and hope warring for dominance.

As Lucy burst outside into the cool night air, she heard her father's furious shout behind her. But she didn't stop. Couldn't stop. Her feet carried her across the lawn, toward the stables, where she knew Clive would be waiting.

The damp grass and mud soaked through her satin slippers, the chill seeping into her bones.

"Please be there," she whispered between ragged breaths. "Please be there."

The stables loomed before her, just as she saw a figure approaching. Her heart hoped it was him, but the closer she became, she knew the form was feminine.

It was Lady Augusta, her elegant frame becoming clearer as she approached. Lucy's heart clenched at the sight of the matron, confused at why she was there and what it all meant.

"Lady Augusta?"

"Oh, my dear girl," Lady Augusta said, her voice thick with sorrow. "He's gone."

Lucy felt as if the ground had disappeared beneath her feet. "Gone? What do you mean, gone?" She stumbled forward, gripping Lady Augusta's arms. "He can't be. He wouldn't leave without—"

"Clive had no choice, Lucy," Lady Augusta interrupted gently, her hazel eyes filled with a mix of sympathy and sorrow. "Your father... he made certain arrangements."

Her chest caved inward. No. No, no, no... Clive's whispered words at the ball returned to her — the quiet desperation in his voice.

"No," she whispered, unwilling to accept what she was hearing. "No, this can't be happening."

Lady Augusta's hand came to rest on Lucy's cheek. "I'm so sorry, my dear. But—"

Lucy jerked away, her eyes wild. "Where did he go? Tell me, please! I'll follow him, I'll—"

"Lucy!" The duke's furious shout pierced the night.

But Lucy barely heard him. All she could focus on was the crushing weight in her chest, the feeling of walls closing in around her. Clive was gone. Her dreams, her hopes, her chance at true happiness—all vanished in the night.

She sank to her knees, the mud soaking through her pristine white gown. Apparently her father was right, she had ended up in the mud after all.

"No," she whispered, her voice breaking on his name.

Lucy's fingers dug into the soft, wet earth, mud seeping beneath her fingernails as she fought to gain control over herself.

"Lucy, for heaven's sake, get up this instant!" Her mother's shrill voice cut through the air. "You're making a spectacle of yourself! And you've ruined your gown."

But Lucy remained motionless, her body trembling with barely contained emotion.

"I won't," she whispered, her voice growing stronger with each word. "I won't be your puppet any longer. And I won't marry Rutherford."

Her father stepped closer, his tone a mixture of exasperation and concern. "You're upset, my dear. But this behavior is unbecoming of a lady of your station. Think of what people will say—"

"I don't give a damn!" Lucy cried, rising to her feet with sudden force. "I'm done living the life you expect me to. You don't control me any longer. This ends now."

Lucy moved, so she faced her parents, squaring her shoulders and raising her chin. More confidence than she'd ever felt in her entire life to stand up for herself.

Her father's scowl was even more intimidating in the moonlight, but Lucy held her ground and didn't flinch.

"You will marry Lord Rutherford, or I'll wash my hands of you."

Her mother gasped beside him, clutching his arm in the first display of defiance that Lucy had ever seen from her. "No," she whispered.

"I mean what I say, girl," her father continued. "Clean yourself and sleep on the matter. Come to my study tomorrow morning with your answer. If you choose that...servant, you leave with nothing."

He turned on his heel, storming off. Her mother hesitated, her face pale and uncertain, before following after him.

Lady Augusta moved to comfort Lucy, but Lucy held up a mud-stained hand. "No, please. I need... I need to be alone."

"Lucy," Lady Augusta said, more insistent. "We really must speak."

Lucy eyed the woman curiously. "You know where he went."

"Yes. I sent him to Surrey."

"Why would you send him away?" Lucy couldn't hold back her outburst.

"My dear," Lady Augusta started, then drew a deep breath. "My married name is Augusta Clive. And my late husband was well known for the rate at which he went through willing women, including those he paid."

Lucy shook her head, trying to make sense of how any of this mattered. "Why are you telling me this?"

"Clive, dear. My husband was Clive's father."

"How can you be certain?" And even if it could be confirmed, it changed nothing.

"I discussed the matter with Clive after you took off on your horse. He looks almost exactly like my son. The emerald-green eyes, chestnut hair, masculine jaw...every bit their father, I must say."

"Why did you send him to Surrey?"

"His father was the most prominent horse breeder in England. Followed by my son before he unexpectedly became the Earl of Powis. And Clive deserves the opportunity to help run his family's business."

Her heart deflated. "So he left me so he could take up the business he's always wanted for himself?"

"No, my dear," Augusta said, gripping her shoulders. "All he was concerned about was that he could provide for you. He told me your father had given him the sack with orders to never speak to you again, so I told him to go to Surrey. Clive didn't want to leave without you, but he also didn't want to force your hand. He wanted to give you the chance to stand up to your parents for yourself.

Clive will wait for you there, if a life with him is what you choose."

There wasn't a question in her mind. She didn't need to sleep on it.

"How can I get to him? I have no carriage of my own, so I suppose I shall have to purchase passage on the mail carriage. And I need directions to where to find him. I shall depart in the morning." Lucy stared at Lady Augusta's smiling face. "I must ask you again to not tell anyone. Please, I beg you."

"I'll do better than that," Lady Augusta said, taking Lucy's hands. "I shall take you to him myself. Pack what you wish to carry, and we shall leave at first light."

Lucy hugged her. "Has anyone ever told you that you are meddlesome?"

Lady Augusta laughed, appearing unoffended by the question, hugging her back. "Perhaps."

"And I'm eternally grateful."

Chapter 13

Clive

Clive trudged along the dirt path, the weight of his worn satchel digging into his shoulder. The mail carriage had left him in a nearby village, and he'd walked the rest of the way to Clive House with nothing but thoughts of Lucy and the uncertain road ahead.

His fine clothes, borrowed from a footman at Ashburn Manor for the masquerade, clung uncomfortably to his skin. The expensive fabric now felt like a cruel reminder of how far out of place he'd been — a stable hand masquerading as something more. He'd tossed a few coins to the footman for the garments before fleeing the manor. Had the Duke caught him that night... Clive shook his head. He didn't want to think about what might have happened.

But he had to see Lucy before he left. He'd almost turned back, nearly scaled the manor wall to steal her away, but forced himself forward. Lucy deserved to make her choice freely — without the pressure of a desperate man begging her to run.

The house came into view. Its white stone façade softened by ivy crawling up the walls. Stables sprawled beside the property, larger than any he'd ever seen. A testament to the success of the business his father had built. Hope stirred inside him for the first time in days. Perhaps there was a life for them there.

At the stable doors, Clive paused. Inside, a young man brushed down a magnificent black stallion. Easily eighteen hands high, a striking beast that radiated strength.

"Might I speak to John?" Clive asked.

The man wiped his hands on his trousers and stepped forward. "I'll fetch him. Who should I say is calling?"

"Clive Jones," he replied. "Lady Augusta sent me."

The stable hand nodded and hurried off.

Left alone, Clive absently stroked the stallion's powerful neck. The horse tossed its head, then relaxed under his touch. "Aren't you a beauty," Clive murmured.

"Impressive creature, isn't he?" a deep voice called from behind.

Clive turned to see a man approaching — tall, sandy-haired, and broad-shouldered. His easy gait and weathered face marked him as a man accustomed to long hours working in the sun. He eyed Clive as if he were trying to place how he knew him.

““You must be John,” Clive said, extending his hand. “Lady Augusta sent me to see you. To see about putting me to work.”

John's grip was firm, strong — the kind that demanded respect. “You've experience working with horses?”

“Most of my life,” Clive replied.

John's brow quirked. “Seems a bit odd that my aunt would send you to me. Care to explain how you know her?”

Clive shuffled on his feet, unsure what the man would think about what he had to say. He drew a deep breath and explained the story to his cousin, not leaving out the part of his hope to wed Lucy.

John released a long whistle. “Oh my, that is a tale. And to go for a duke's daughter…you are bold, that is for certain.” John assessed him, squinting as he stared at his face. “You know... I thought you looked familiar. You've got the same sharp features as Graham—my cousin. Your half-brother, I suppose.”

Clive let out a heavy breath. “I doubt an earl will welcome a bastard brother with open arms.”

John chuckled and clasped his shoulder. "I grew up with Graham, and I can assure you that he shall welcome you into the family. And this?" He gestured to the stables and fields stretching beyond, "This has always been a family business."

Clive allowed his shoulders to relax for the first time in hours. He wasn't certain how he had been so fortunate to discover his family, and that they might even welcome and embrace him.

"Come with me," John said, nodding toward the back exit. "Let's get you into some different clothing and then I'll show you around."

They walked to John's home, where Clive was given fresh clothes. Fortunately, he and John were around the same size.

When they returned to the stables, Clive fell into step beside his cousin touring everything the family had built.

Pausing before a stall, Clive found himself face to face with a striking bay stallion. The horse tossed its head, nostrils flaring as it eyed him.

"This one reminds me of Lucy's horse," Clive murmured, extending his hand. The stallion stretched its neck, warm breath ghosting over Clive's palm before nuzzling against him.

"You really love her," John said quietly.

Clive's hand stilled. "More than anything." His voice was thick. "I'm not sure what I'll do if she doesn't come."

"If my aunt told you Lucy would follow," John said with quiet confidence, "then I'd wager she knows what she's talking about."

Hope ignited in his chest. He could already imagine a life with Lucy there, free to love each other as they wished.

"I've never had a proper home before," Clive said, more to himself than to John. But even in the short time there, that's already what he'd felt. That he'd finally found a home. And all that was missing was Lucy.

John clapped a hand to his shoulder. "Well, you've got one now."

For the rest of the afternoon, they worked side by side, and with each passing hour, Clive felt more at ease. John told stories of Clive's father and brother, giving him a better sense of who they were. For the first time in his life, Clive felt a connection to something bigger. A place where he belonged.

As they finished the last of the day's tasks, Clive turned to his cousin. "Thank you," he said. "For everything."

"You're family," John replied with a smile. "And I'm glad you found us, or Aunt found you, rather. Besides, I've been lonely with Graham off tending to his duties as an earl now."

"You don't have to worry about that with me. Once Lucy arrives…if she arrives, I'm uncertain I'll ever have cause to leave." Assuming she did, in fact, arrive.

"She'll come," John said firmly. "Mark my words."

Clive nodded, but his heart still ached with uncertainty. He stared at the road, willing her to appear.

And he knew—he wouldn't feel whole again until she did.

Chapter 14

Clive

It had been three days.

Three long, heartbreaking days since Clive had arrived in Surrey. Three days spent convincing himself that Lucy was simply delayed — that she was gathering what she needed, making her plans. But by the third morning, hope had begun to sour into dread. Perhaps her father had discovered her intentions. Perhaps she was being held against her will.

Perhaps she had changed her mind.

The uncertainty gnawed at him, turning his thoughts to restless turmoil. He worked harder than ever, throwing himself into training the powerful black stallion that John had gifted him. Come to find out, Clive's brother had the horse's brother, Midnight, as his own mount.

The physical labor kept his body busy, but his mind refused to quiet.

If she didn't arrive by the following day, he would return for her. He never should have left her. And his heart couldn't take much longer of not knowing.

The distant creak of carriage wheels cut through his thoughts.

Clive stilled, heart pounding so fiercely he feared it might shake him apart. His breath hitched as he turned toward the sound, his gaze locking on the road.

"Easy now," he murmured, as much to himself as to the horse, who trotted around him.

As the carriage rolled closer and drew to a halt, Clive found himself rooted to the spot, scarcely daring to breathe.

Then she appeared.

Lucy stepped down from the carriage. Her blue eyes swept the yard, searching, until they locked with his. The world belonged only to the two of them, everything else fading away.

"Lucy," Clive breathed.

She took a step toward him, her lips curving into a radiant smile that sent a jolt of electricity through his entire being.

Without another thought, Clive vaulted over the fence. In three long strides, he reached Lucy, scooping her into his arms.

He crushed her against him, one hand tangling in her hair while the other cupped her face. His lips claimed hers in a desperate kiss. Fierce, hungry, as if he could pour every moment of agony, of waiting, into that single act.

Her arms wound tightly around his neck, her mouth parting eagerly beneath his. The taste of her, warm and sweet, was everything he had craved.

When he finally pulled back, they were both breathless. He pressed his forehead to hers, fighting to steady his voice. "I was about to come for you," he whispered.

Lucy's fingers tightened in his hair, her smile teasing. "Does that mean you missed me?"

"More than you could ever know."

Lady Augusta stepped out of the carriage and caught their attention, observing their reunion. "I am delighted for you both," she sighed contentedly, her eyes twinkling when she grinned at Clive.

"We would have been here sooner," Lucy continued. "But we broke an axle and had to await the repair."

"I had to keep her from walking here in her desperation to get to you," Lady Augusta said, shaking her head, but her tone was laced with mirth. "Perhaps you might continue this reunion somewhere more... private?"

Clive felt his cheeks flush, aware of their very public display. But as he looked down at Lucy, seeing the love and certainty shining in her eyes, he found he couldn't bring himself to care what anyone might think. In that moment, with the woman he loved in his arms and the promise of a future together, that was all that mattered.

Clive gazed into Lucy's eyes, his heart thundering in his chest. "Lucy," he breathed, his voice husky with emotion. "I can't wait another moment."

Before Lucy could speak, he dropped to one knee, his hand trembling as he reached for hers. Lucy gasped, her fingers flying to her lips, her eyes wide with surprise.

"You deserve everything your heart desires," Clive said, his voice shaking. "And I swear to you, Lucy Lygon, no man on this earth could love you more fiercely or completely than I do. I will spend every day of my life loving you, protecting you, and building a life worthy of you." His voice broke slightly. "Please... marry me."

For a heartbeat, the world seemed to still. His heart pounded so loudly he was certain she must hear it.

Then Lucy let out a breathless, tearful laugh. "Oh, Clive," she whispered, falling to her knees and throwing her arms around him. "Yes! You are all I shall ever need."

Joy exploded inside him as Clive urged them to their feet and swept her into his arms, spinning her in a giddy circle that left them both breathless with laughter.

"I love you," he whispered fiercely, setting her to her feet before he kissed her again. "I love you so much."

"We must find the quickest way to wed," Clive said, his voice thick with emotion. "I can't bear to spend another night without you."

Clive rested his forehead against hers, overwhelmed by the depth of his emotions. "We must determine the fastest way to wed."

"You just leave all of that to me," Lady Augusta declared, wiping a tear from her eye.

He took Lucy's hand in his, pressing a kiss to her fingers. "I'll never let you go," he vowed.

"You'd better not."

Clive looped his arm around Lucy's waist, trailing behind Lady Augusta to the house. He fought the urge to pinch himself, because his every dream had come true.

Epilogue

1 YEAR LATER: LUCY

Lucy stood on the terrace of Clive House, the home she had shared with her husband for the past year. Lady Augusta had insisted they live there since no one was in residence, and John has his own home on the ground. After much convincing, Clive had relented. It was a grand house, yet cozy in a way that felt like home — a feeling Lucy had never known until she fell in love with Clive.

She leaned on the railing, one hand pressed to the soft swell of her belly. Her other hand lingered over her heart as she watched Clive work a young horse in the paddock. The horse showed promise as a racehorse and would fetch a small fortune. Lucy had never fully appreciated how expensive horses were and what members of the ton were willing to pay for a well-bred horse.

Thunder rumbled low in the distance, the scent of rain thickening the air. The darkening clouds mirrored the storm that had once defined their relationship — a relentless push and pull, love fighting against duty, their passion tempered by impossible odds. Yet here they were now, stronger, happier, and still just as consumed with each other as the day they'd met.

Life had been quite comfortable. They'd never needed to touch the funds from her inheritance, as they made more than enough to live on with Clive's share of the business. Instead, they'd invested her inheritance to grow their wealth for their future children.

Lucy smiled, remembering their conversation the night before. Clive had been fretting, as he so often did lately, about her condition, insisting she rest more. In truth, she didn't mind a bit of rest, but she missed taking the horses out for a ride with her husband. Thor seemed to miss their daily rides as well, and Lucy still visited her beloved horse every day. Her parents had sent him to her months after she left, in their attempt to make amends.

A footman interrupted her thoughts. He extended a sealed letter, her father's crest glaring from the wax. Lucy's stomach twisted, but she accepted it and broke the seal. The words made her breath catch. Her parents had accepted her invitation to visit.

She had extended the olive branch to them after they expressed their desire to reconcile. Her brother gave them an earful when he arrived back from his extended grand tour and learned of what had occurred.

Lucy and Clive had discussed the matter at length before she'd offered. She'd made it clear to them they must respect her husband or there would be no need for them to visit at all. Margot and her husband would also come, so they would help ensure Lucy's parents behaved.

As complicated as her relationship had been with her parents, she'd like for them to get to know the woman she truly was and not the one they tried to make her become.

Seeing how Graham, the Earl of Powis, had welcomed Clive into his life, left her optimistic. Not that she was entirely surprised that Graham had done so. She knew his wife, Diana, and their friends from when she attended ton events, and they were all known for love matches, as well as skirting many of their society's rules. Clive had been uncomfortable interacting with so many titled gentlemen at first, but they'd made him feel welcome and hadn't treated him any differently.

Her focus shifted back to Clive. The mere sight of him still had the power to take her breath away. Every. Single.

Time. He worked hard and was the most loving, attentive husband every day of their marriage.

Before the doctor confirmed the impending arrival of their babe, she worked alongside him and John, learning to train the horses. She had the idea to make their stables a location where women could apprentice. John and Clive expressed unwavering support, so while Clive urged her to rest, she worked on the plans for how to organize the program.

Thunder roared, and she glanced at the sky, finding dark, ominous clouds. She watched as Clive hurried the horse into the stables. A few moments later, raindrops fell, and Lucy enjoyed the cool feel of the rain against her skin. Clive raced up the stairs of the terrace.

"We must get you inside, my love," he said, pressing a tender kiss to her brow, the hair on his forehead damp.

She didn't move, wrapping her arms around his waist, as the rain picked up and fell in sheets.

"Remember the last time we found ourselves caught in a storm?"

His eyes shone with immense love. "I shall never forget it."

She pressed up on her toes, giving her husband a light kiss, then licked along his bottom lip before she gave it a small nibble. "What if I required a bit of reminding?"

Clive released a low growl, then swept her up to cradle her in his arms. "I hope you have nothing else planned today, because I'm going to remind you several times."

Lucy kicked her feet in delight and wrapped her arms around his neck. She could never get enough of her husband.

He carried her just inside to a small parlor, locking the door behind him before setting her on the settee. Her husband went to work pulling off his shirt, and the sight of his bare chest always drove her mad.

Before she could stop herself, she was on her knees in front of him, tugging at his breeches. "I suddenly find I remember a few things." She unfastened the buttons of his falls, freeing his cock from the confines of his breeches.

"Sweetheart, I can't have my pregnant wife—" Lucy swirled her tongue around the head of his cock "—oh, fuck."

She grinned and then took him deeper into her mouth, sucking hard, reveling in the sounds she elicited from her husband. "What was that, my love?" she teased, and then sucked his member as far into her mouth as she could.

"That feels so good, Wife. Have your fun, but I have every intention of finishing inside of you."

She bobbed her head on his cock, her core heating from the wicked way her husband tasted. Clive moaned and shifted his hands to grip her head, moving against her mouth at his own pace.

"Touch yourself," he ground out, staring down at her. "Make yourself moan on my cock."

Bunching her skirts, she worked her hand between her legs, circling her pearl. Moaning as she increased the intensity of how hard she sucked him.

She continued, driving herself close to the peak of her climax, from where she massaged her own sensitive flesh while pleasuring her husband.

"Look at me," he called to her, almost breathless.

Lucy fixed her gaze on his, and the electricity of the moment almost finished her. He groaned again when she sucked him harder.

"Enough," he ground out, pulling his cock from her mouth.

He picked her up and set her bottom on the edge of the nearby desk, and knelt in front of her, sucking her pearl. She was already far too close, and before she could stop herself, her thighs squeezed tight against the sides of his head when her orgasm took over.

Before she had time to think or recover, he gripped her again at her hips. He lifted her as if she were light as a feather, pulling her against him so she could wrap her legs around his waist.

Clive guided himself inside of her, walking her to the wall between two large windows. The storm raged outside, and it was no match for the intensity of her husband bucking into her with her back against the wall.

"God, you feel so good, Lucy," he ground out.

The way he moved his hips stoked her perfectly, and she fought to breathe from the intensity of the pleasure, knowing that it was building to something even more exquisite. She fought it was long as she could, but when he brought her to the height of ecstasy again, she gripped his shoulders, digging her fingernails into his skin and wrapping her legs tighter around him as she crested, moaning so loud, their servants surely would have heard.

"That's it," he growled, pumping into her twice more before he slowed as he filled her.

He took her lips with his, the kiss slow and tender. A stark contrast to how untamed he'd just been. Clive walked them over to the settee, his lips not leaving hers, and sat down so she straddled his lap while he kissed her.

After several moments, Lucy broke the kiss and pulled back to gaze at him. "I love you. That was wonderful."

He smirked at her. "I love you most. But enjoy your rest, Sweetheart, because I am far from finished with you."

"Please tell me we shall always be like this," she sighed, laying against him.

"Does that mean you don't regret leaving your life of balls and ton gossip for the likes of me?"

She nuzzled his neck, the intoxicating smell of his skin consuming her senses. "You do know the gossip sheets are delivered here, don't you?"

He laughed and kissed her forehead. "I always dreamed of a life like this. What we have matters more to me than anything. I would live in the mud if it meant I could have you."

"I feel quite the same. But obviously, I realized it before you did," she teased, then her expression turned serious.

A crack of lightning illuminated the entire room, followed by a loud boom of thunder.

"Enough talking," Clive said, settling Lucy on her back on the settee. "The only thing I wish to hear from your lips is my name."

And that was all she had to say for the rest of the afternoon, and late into the evening. Repeatedly.

Want more Lucy and Clive? Join my newsletter for an additional scene of Lucy and Clive in their married life and the start of Lucy's apprenticeship! Check it out here: https://dl.bookfunnel.com/fj5s56jns2

Also enjoy this freebie novella from me: https://dl.bookfunnel.com/a8gorf3mjj

Be sure to continue onto the next few pages for a sneak peek at The Earl and the Vixen, too!

Dearest Reader

Thank you for taking the time to read *Their Forbidden Storm*! I hope you enjoyed this spicy read! You'll get to see Graham Clive and his cousin John again soon when my Romancing the Ton Series releases starting fall 2025!

For an introduction to my Unlikely Betrothal series, join my newsletter to get your free copy of *The Viscount and the Minx*, a prequel novella leading up to a scandalous house party that serves as the setting for five couples to meet their match!

I am so thankful for all my readers and would appreciate it if you would leave an honest review on sites like Amazon, Goodreads, BookBub, etc.! Also, I'd love to stay in touch, so please visit christinadianebooks.com to join my mailing list and stay informed on upcoming releases, promotions, and current projects.

If you are interested in being on my permanent ARC team and/or Street Team, send me a message on one of my socials! I'd love to chat!

I hope all of you will follow me and get the latest happenings and info on releases from my historical romance friends on any of my socials:

- Website: christinadianebooks.com
- Substack: @christinadianeauthor
- The Desire Den Discord
- Instagram: @christinadianeauthor
- Facebook: christinadiane
- TikTok: @christinadianeauthor
- YouTube: @ChristinaDianeAuthor
- BlueSky: @christinadiane.bsky.social
- Twitter: @CDianeAuthor
- GoodReads: ChristinaDiane
- Follow Me onBookBub: Christina Diane

- Join my Reader Group: The Swoonworthy Scoundrels Society
- Join my other Author Group: Society of Smut & Scandal

Hopefully I left you wanting more, so keep reading for a sneak peek at the first book, *The Earl and the Vixen,* from the Unlikely Betrothal series! I can't wait for you to meet Nick and Eliza! You can also go ahead and get your copy of *The Earl and the Vixen* in paperback, ebook, and audio!

CHRISTINA
DIANE

The Earl and the Vixen

SURREY, ENGLAND - SPRING 1810

"I love you, Eliza, and I intend to marry you. To hell with our fathers. Please tell me you want to be with me as much as I wish to be with you. In every way."

Elizabeth Nelson, the eldest daughter of the Earl of Nelson, melted into the arms of her sweetheart, Nicholas, who would one day become the Earl of Craven. She had loved him from the first time she'd come across him swimming in the stream that ran between their fathers' estates, almost five years ago.

Although the ownership of that very stream had been a long-disputed issue between their fathers. They each believed that the stream belonged to them and made trouble for each other when either household made use of it for livestock or to provide irrigation to crops. Ultimately, they both ended up using it for their estates anyway, and one would think they could be content with that. But a silly stream had been enough to cause such a rift that the men had sworn to hate each other. The bad blood only became worse between the pair over the years.

When she first saw Nick all those years ago, he hadn't given one whit about her back then. She had been far too young, and he had only been home for the summer from Eton, and by the time fall came again, he was gone. When he returned years later, he came across her reading a novel by the very same stream and finally noticed her, a woman and no longer an annoying young chit. They spent the next few months falling more in love each day and taking a few scandalous swims together at night in the stream in a rebellious slight against their fathers.

There wasn't a doubt in her mind that she wished to marry him, and she wanted nothing more than to give him every part of herself. To truly become his and make him hers. As a young woman of eight-and-ten whom no one spoke of such things to, she knew very little of what that would mean, but she knew she only wished to experience such things with Nick.

He would have offered to marry her already, and they would already be betrothed if they knew for certain how their fathers would react. Given the hatred the men harbored for each other, they feared that Eliza's father wouldn't agree to the union. With her age, they needed his approval to do so properly, or they would have to do something scandalous like elope to Gretna Green.

"I love you, too," she said, burying her face in his neck. "I want very much to be with you, Nick."

He took her mouth with his, kissing her with fervent intensity. When he broke the kiss, he brought her hands to his swollen lips. "Meet me at the hunting cabin tonight, after it is dark. We can be alone there, just the two of us with no one to disturb us."

She looked at their hands, attempting to mask her frown.

"What is it, Eliza? If you have doubts, we can wait," Nick said. He lifted her chin to meet his mesmerizing green eyes. His chestnut hair was just a bit longer than was fashionable, and it made him all the more roguish and handsome. "Look at me. I mean it, if this isn't something you wish to do—"

"It's not that," she said, cutting him off.

"Then is it something I have done? Did you not enjoy when I touched you…" his voice trailed off as he gestured towards her skirts.

"It is most certainly not that either," she said before swallowing hard. She had quite enjoyed it when he introduced her to the most exquisite pleasure she had ever experienced. "It's just that I know you have experienced these things before, and I haven't a clue what to expect or what to do."

Nick had always been honest with her, and he told her of his time at Cambridge and that there had been women who warmed his bed. He spared her the details, which she appreciated, but she wasn't so secure in herself that it didn't spark a flicker of jealousy, especially when she was about to lay herself bare before him.

She knew that the rules of society were different for men than women, especially since Nick was two-and-twenty and exposed to the things men do while at university, but it didn't mean she had to like it.

He cupped her cheek with his hand. "My love, you will be perfect. All I need is you. The rest we can explore together."

"But you—"

"Nothing that happened before you matters," he said, cutting her off, "and I know it isn't fair for me to say so, but I would be driven mad if I had to imagine even the mere notion of another man touching you. If I could change the past, I promise you, I would. Just know that it is of little import to me. You are my future. My everything."

She pressed onto her toes and kissed him again. "I will meet you tonight. I shall have to wait until after Papa goes to bed if I hope to leave." Her papa would not approve of her sneaking out to meet any man, let alone the son of the Earl of Craven. He might have apoplexy if he knew she intended to give Nick her virtue. Papa tolerated Nick's presence when he came to call only because of the politeness society expected. She was certain Papa would refuse him if it wouldn't upset Eliza. Perhaps when she and Nick married, their fathers might resolve things between them. One could only hope.

He brought her hand to his lips again and kissed her knuckles. "You had better return home before someone comes looking for us," he said. "I will see you tonight, my love."

She took his lips again for a few quick pecks and peeked around the corner from the back of her family's stables, ensuring no one could see her as she hurried back towards the house. Her father might tolerate Nick visiting for tea, but if he caught her with him unchaperoned, she wasn't certain she'd see the light of day again. They had to get creative to find ways to sneak off without her maid in tow.

Eliza made it back to the terrace of her grand country home without anyone taking notice. As soon as she entered, she almost walked straight into her father.

"Where have you been, daughter?" he asked.

"I was just taking in the air in the garden, Papa," she lied. She didn't enjoy lying to her father, but she couldn't have him locking her away in her room. Surely love was a reason to justify the minor sin.

His brow furrowed, assessing her. "Where is your maid? You shouldn't be roaming the grounds alone."

"You are quite right, Papa. I just stepped out for a few moments after I was tired of reading. I will make sure Dot goes with me next time," she said, hoping her father wouldn't press her any further.

"Very well. See that you do. Did that boy call here today?"

"Nick?" she asked.

Her father nodded. "And shouldn't you refer to him as Lord Craven?" Hate spewed when her father spoke the title. "You aren't on familiar terms."

Eliza opted not to point out that her father should also refer to Nick by his title and not "that boy," but she opted to leave that unsaid. "Papa, he isn't his father and has done nothing to you. And no, he didn't," she replied. It wasn't exactly a lie since he didn't come calling to their door. "Perhaps he will come for tea tomorrow."

"You are to depart for town with your mama in a few weeks for the season. You are certain to marry before the season ends, so there isn't much point in the boy calling here, I should think," he said, his lips curled into a smirk.

"Perhaps he will offer for me and save you the expense of a season, Papa," she said, testing the waters for her father's reaction.

If she hoped to find a hint of his thoughts on her statement, she would be disappointed. His expression remained unchanged, other than a slight squint of his eyes.

"Perhaps," he said, "but you would have many acceptable options if you had a season."

She patted her father's arm. "The most important thing is that I marry someone who loves me, right, Papa?"

"And someone who is respectable and comes from an excellent family. Someone who would ensure you are provided for," her father said, his cool expression still unchanged.

"Of course, Papa," she replied. "I should like to return to the new book I just purchased with my pin money. May I be excused?" She wasn't ready to tell her father she had already made her choice and would marry Nick. Even if she had to run away with him to Gretna, he was the man she would marry, and there wasn't a thing her father could do about it.

"See you at dinner," her father said before departing towards his study.

Eliza continued to her room, unable to concentrate on reading as her heart wouldn't stop racing. She couldn't wait for her rendezvous with Nick later that evening, where she would learn what it meant to couple with the man she loved.

Around eleven o'clock, Eliza poked her head out of her room to see if anyone was lurking in the hallway. Dot had dressed her for bed a couple hours ago and set her hair into a long plait held in place with a ribbon before she sent the maid away for the evening. Eliza slipped on a serviceable day dress over her night rail and then covered herself with a pelisse to help keep from catching a chill in the cool night air.

Once she was certain there was no one moving about the house, she slipped out of her room and closed the door behind her. She made her way downstairs and snuck out via the door the servants used to access the kitchen garden.

The hunting cabin was only a ten-minute swift ride away, and she knew the route well. With a confident smile, she set off on the journey, assured of her safety under the luminous full moon. She crept to the mews, and a groom greeted her.

"Please saddle up my horse and tell no one that you saw me," she said, handing him a couple of coins.

He pocketed the coins and set off to do as she asked. Jimmy had done so for her a few times before, when she would sneak out to see Nick. The last time they snuck to the hunting cabin, she learnt what an orgasm was. Who knew that a man's hands could give such pleasure? She clenched her thighs together, already thinking about what delights he would introduce her to that evening.

A few moments later, Jimmy handed her the reins, positioning the horse by the mounting block. She thanked him and climbed into the saddle before flicking the reins and racing off into the night.

When she reached the cabin, Nick's horse was already tied up outside. He waited on the porch for her and came right beside her horse and lifted her down. "I'm so very glad you made it, my love. I would have preferred to escort you," Nick said, pulling her into an embrace for a quick kiss. "Let's get you inside. I already started a fire for us."

She grabbed his hand, and he led her inside. The warmth from the fire kissed her skin right away. She removed her pelisse and laid it across the back of the settee. She turned to face him, and in a single fluid movement, he swept her into his arms. Nick pressed his lips to hers, running his tongue along her bottom lip before her lips parted and he massaged her tongue with his. She returned his kiss, sucking his tongue into her mouth until he groaned.

He ambled her backward towards the bedchamber, not breaking their kiss, which grew wilder by the moment. Once inside the room, he kissed her jaw and neck, nibbling at her and then soothing the nips with his tongue.

Eliza sighed, loving the man before her more than she could have thought possible. She glanced around the room and noted he had started a fire in the bedchamber as well, and there were a few candles lit on the mantle above the fireplace.

Nick took her hands in his and leaned back to look at her. His expression was an intoxicating mixture of need and love, and with the light from fire casting shadows on his handsome face, it was an image depicted right out of one of her romance novels. His chestnut hair was almost black in the low lighting and the candlelight hit his green eyes just perfectly so that they shone like a precious gem. She lost her heart to him all over again.

"Are you certain you wish to do this?" he asked, placing a soft kiss on her jaw.

"More than anything," she replied. They had talked about waiting until they were married, but the desire to be with him had consumed her. She couldn't wait for her father to approve her choice. She needed to be with him in every way, and then they would fight for their future together.

A low growl escaped his lips, and he began working the buttons of her dress, unfastening enough that he could lift it over her head and then tossed it on the chair beside the bed.

Curious about what Nick would look like without his clothing, she unbuttoned the coat he wore and pushed it off his shoulders until it fell to the floor. She worked the buttons of his white shirt next. He remained still and allowed her to do as she wished, staring into her eyes as she undid each button and freed him from his shirt.

Her breath caught when she saw his muscular chest with a light smattering of dark hair. When she ran her hands across chiseled muscles and over his shoulders, he sucked in a breath, and the nerves she had about coupling with him evaporated, leaving only raw desire. She kissed his chest, becoming wanton and bold with each press of her lips to his skin. She used her tongue in the same way he did against her neck, and his muscles flexed beneath her touch.

"Eliza, that feels so good."

She licked and kissed his collarbone and up his neck, finding the lobe of his ear. She sucked it into her mouth.

He grabbed her head and kissed her lips again. After a few moments of exploration with their tongues, he broke the kiss and pulled her night rail over her head, leaving her naked before him.

She watched his response to her, and the hunger in his eyes only emboldened her further.

"You are so beautiful," he said, looking from her breasts and down her body. "I must taste you."

She wasn't sure what he meant, but he clasped her bottom and lifted her onto the bed. He tenderly laid her down across the massive bed and positioned himself on his knees between her legs.

He kissed her lips, then kissed his way to her breasts. Her entire body shivered from the sensation of his powerful form hovering over her and the anticipation of what he would do. She gasped when he took one of her nipples into his mouth and began suckling her. "Nick," she cried out.

"Do you like this?" he asked, stopping what he was doing.

"Oh, yes," she replied.

He dipped his head to continue, smiling against her breast every time she moaned or sucked in a breath.

When he used his hand to find her nub in the nest of curls between her legs, she moaned again.

He released her nipple and kissed his way down her stomach. He kissed lower and lower, shifting himself further down on the bed until his head was between her legs.

"What are you—" She cried out when his tongue flicked her pearl. "God, yes," she moaned.

He stopped and glanced up at her, a smirk playing on his lips. "Does that mean you wish for me to continue?"

"I may never wish for you to stop."

He gave a smug laugh and flicked her pearl again before circling it with his tongue. He inserted a finger into her core and moved it in and out. Her hands flew to his head, and she undulated against his mouth and hand.

She approached a release similar to the one he gave her a couple of nights ago with his hand, but this was different. Far more intense and wicked. When she tipped over the edge of her climax, she rocked and moaned, calling out his name.

He shifted himself on top of her and kissed her lips. She tasted herself on his tongue and licked the wetness off his lips. It was erotic and exhilarating, and she knew that once would never be enough.

"I could drink from you all day," he said.

"I may wish for you to do just that." She giggled when he laughed at her declaration. "I didn't know such a thing was possible," she said.

He kissed her again. "Would you like to stop now, or would you like for me to show you more?"

"I want more," she replied, the need evident in her tone. "Please, Nick."

Nick climbed off the bed and stood beside it, looking at her.

"Where are you going?" she asked, curving her lips in a playful pout.

"I must remove these now," he replied, working the buttons of his falls, his eyes not leaving hers. He pushed his breeches down to the floor and his member sprang to life, protruding from a nest of dark curls. Her gaze fixed on it, curious about what it might feel like in her hand.

He climbed back onto the bed and hovered over her, placing another sweet kiss on her lips.

"I want to touch you," she said, reaching between them to grasp the rod that stood erect between them.

He sucked in a large breath and closed his eyes when her hand closed around it. Balancing himself with one hand and his knees, he reached his free hand between them and wrapped it around hers. His cock was smooth to the touch but hard as steel.

"You can stroke me like this." He moved her hand with his, and she loved the power she felt from giving him pleasure the way he did for her.

She continued to stroke him for a few moments before he pulled her hand away. "I will spend if you should continue, and I would much rather do so after I make you come on my cock."

She bit her lip, enjoying his wicked words. "Tell me what you are going to do and don't be polite about it."

He slipped his hand between them and slid two fingers inside of her. "I'm going to replace my fingers with the head of my aching shaft, and then I'm going to move like this"—he slid his fingers in and out—"until you shatter and moan in my arms."

She released a sound that was a mixture of a sign and a moan. He pressed his lips to her ear. "Do you want me inside you now?" he whispered.

She nodded.

"Tell me you want me to make love to you with my needy cock," he said, kissing along her jaw.

"I want your cock, Nick," she whispered. "Make love to me. Now."

He withdrew his fingers and positioned himself at her opening. "This may hurt but not for long, and it shouldn't do so ever again."

He pushed himself into her with care, inch by inch. She gasped from the slight twinge of pain when he had his entire length inside of her.

"Are you all right?" he asked.

"Yes," she whispered, the pain subsiding, and she had the urge to move against him. "It doesn't hurt any longer."

He withdrew and then thrust back inside of her, causing her to see stars. She had never imagined such a pleasure and reveled in the intimacy from the man she loved most in the world filling her, the two of them joining as one. Nothing and no one else mattered but the two of them. He did it again, and she cried out.

"That's it, my love. Moan as loud as you wish. It drives me wild to hear you do so."

With every moan, he thrust deeper and harder inside of her. She wrapped her legs around him, and it became even more intense when he entered her as far as he could. He panted and groaned, and she pushed herself against him to meet his thrusts.

"You are mine," he said, thrusting hard and deep.

She responded with a loud moan and dug her fingers into his back.

"Say it," he whispered against her lips.

Eliza kissed him and broke the kiss to speak. "I am yours," she said. "I shall always be yours."

He thrust into her harder and faster.

"Oh, yes," she cried out. "Just like that. Don't stop." With each movement, she neared ever closer to madness and ecstasy. "Nick," she moaned.

He didn't relent and made good on his promise to make her shatter. When she did, she cried out his name again and bucked beneath him, arching her back. Once she rode every wave of the intense pleasure from her climax, he withdrew, his breath ragged. "God, Eliza," he groaned before warm liquid pooled on her stomach.

After a few moments, Nick climbed from the bed and removed a handkerchief from his pocket. He wiped between her legs, then her stomach, and set the handkerchief on the table beside the bed.

"I wiped away the blood, but you may be sore tomorrow. A warm bath should help," he said, settling in next to her and pulling her into his arms.

"That was more wonderful than I imagined," she said, brushing his hair away from his face. "I hope it was the same for you."

He pulled her tighter against him. "My love, I have never experienced anything as intense as being with you. I fear I am addicted to you and shall never get enough."

She giggled beside him. "Is that so?"

"It's perfect since you are mine," he said, kissing her forehead.

“Does that mean you shall meet me here tomorrow night and show me more?” she asked, placing a quick kiss on his chest.

“Nothing on this earth could keep me away.”

The Earl and the Vixen is available now: https://christinadianebooks.com/my-books/unlikely-betrothal-series/the-earl-and-the-vixen/

Acknowledgments

There are so many incredible people—both new and longtime ride-or-dies—who have supported me on this wild writing journey. Authors, readers, friends, family, co-workers... you know who you are. I'd list every one of you if I had a few extra pages (and a really small font). Just know this: I adore you, and I'm endlessly grateful.

Steve: My husband, tech wizard, idea bouncer, chef, laundry hero, and all-around MVP. You believe in my big, bold dreams even when they sound like total chaos. Thank you for being my partner in every possible way. Love you, babe.

Dexter and Felix: My boys, my chaos gremlins, and the source of many laughs. You're excellent at distracting me mid-sentence, but you're also the inspiration behind some of the snarky sibling banter that sneaks into my books. One day you'll realize your mom writes smut... and I'll probably owe you both ice cream and therapy. Love you forever.

Rachel, Nina & Brittany: My mom, aunt, and sister—aka my built-in cheer squad. You've supported me through every high, low, and harebrained idea I've ever chased. You hold all my most embarrassing stories, so let's make sure you never talk to anyone without legal counsel present. I love you all dearly.

Erin: From the moment fate brought us together in the most unexpected way, we knew we were meant to be besties. Thank you for listening to every rant, dream, plot twist in life, and meltdown—and for always helping me find my way back to joy and clarity. You're pure magic.

Courtney: Fate handed me a twin flame in the author world. We literally finish each other's sentences (or just say the same thing) and have become legit besties. I can't wait for the day we meet in person. Thank you for our pretty much all day, every day chats, late-night idea storms, the pep talks, and all the chaos we've embraced together. We've got this, twinsie!

Morgan: The magic behind the scenes! You keep everything running, offer genius-level input, and somehow make it all feel easier and more fun. This book—and honestly, this business—wouldn't be the same without you. Thank you, thank you, thank you.

Bliss: Who knew a smutty follow train on Insta would bring me one of my dearest friendsies? Thank you for the endless texts, laughter, spicy scene brainstorming, feedback on my chaos, and all-around moral support. So lucky we found each other!

Rachel: You've read just about everything I've ever written, cheered me on, and gotten delightfully deep into this universe. Thank you for your thoughtful feedback and unwavering encouragement. So happy to have you on this journey.

To my **ARC and Street Team**: Your love, feedback, and support make my heart full. Thank you for shouting about these stories from the rooftops—you make this adventure feel like a party I never want to leave.

To **Dragonblade Publishing:** Thank you for believing in me and my words. I'm so excited to grow alongside such a passionate and supportive team, and be among your esteemed group of authors.

And to all the amazing **author friends** and **influencers** I've met through social media: You're one of the best, most unexpected blessings of this entire journey. Thank you for the inspiration, the laughs, the advice—and most of all, for welcoming me into this magical community.

About the Author

Christina Diane is an award-winning, bestselling author who loves to write super spicy, fast paced stories for the modern reader in the genres of historical romance and dark romance. Her historical romances are all set in the Regency era, with creative liberty taken within the historical setting to create a passionate, hot, intriguing story. Across all of her works, if you love combinations of high spice, witty banter, spirited heroines, forbidden romances, darker themes, and hot alpha men…then you are in for a treat! Because bad boys never go out of style!

She is a hybrid indie and traditionally published author with Dragonblade Publishing, Romance Cafe, and And

You Press. She reads mostly spicy Regency romances and all shades of dark romances, as well as thrillers.

Christina lives in Northern Maine with her husband and two boys. Her family also includes their three French bulldogs who go everywhere with them, as well as two solid black cats. The entire family is always up for new adventures. When she is not writing or chasing after her family, she usually has a Kindle in her hand!

Her writing journey began at the age of nine when she created her own comic strip, Grizzly Grouch. In adulthood, she was a freelance writer for several years, mostly writing lifestyle pieces for blogs. She found that she couldn't stop thinking about stories and characters, so much that she had to get them on the page! Christina frequently has dreams of random character ARCs that go into a massive list of planned writings. She currently has more than ten series just waiting to be written!

Aside from her family, writing, and books, she loves Bridgerton, the Grinch, Jessica Rabbit, horror movies, Chucky dolls, cold brew, yoga, Hamilton, the color pink, and speaking in obscure quotes from movies and TV shows.

Christina loves chatting with her readers and talking about great reads, so please contact her on socials! She'd love to hear what you think about her books and what you'd love to see more of!

Printed in Dunstable, United Kingdom

72525060R00088